SUSAN LUTE

Jane's Long March Home

Falling For a Hero

Cover Design: The Killion Group, Inc.

First edition

ISBN: 978-0-9909607-0-6

This book was professionally typeset on Reedsy.
Find out more at reedsy.com

It takes a village. My village is too cool for words.

Most of all this book is dedicated to David, whose unwavering love and support has not dimmed one iota over the years; to Darren, who saw promise and opportunity when I couldn't; to Damon, who shares my wanderlust and reckless spirit; to Sari, whose heart soars and dreams alongside mine; and especially to Alexis and Dakota, who will be the next generation to go out into the wilderness and conquer.

I love you all!

Jane, a marine fighting to stay with the only family she knows and Chase, a therapist who's lost faith in his ability to help his clients, come together in a moving story of the healing power of kids ... and love. Keep the tissues close at hand!

~ Amazon Review

Amazing story finding love is never easy and finding it can be awesome. Two lost souls along with two children who have lost so much become a true family. Great read do not miss this one

~ Amazon Review

Contents

Foreword

Gunnery Sergeant Jane Donovan's world shatters when a split-second decision in Madrid costs an orphaned child their life. Facing disciplinary action and the possible end of her military career, she's given a final chance: work with Dr. Chase Russell or walk away from the only life she's ever known.

Dr. Chase Russell—once a top trauma counselor, now a reluctant rancher in Central Oregon—is chasing a book deal on PTSD therapies for veterans. But he's still running from his own ghosts. When Jane arrives, battle-scarred and resistant to help, he wants nothing to do with her.

Thrown together by circumstance and two runaway kids, their uneasy alliance deepens through the quiet magic of play therapy and the slow unraveling of secrets long buried. As old wounds resurface and new bonds form, Jane must choose: return to the life she fought so hard for, or take a risk on something entirely different.

And Chase? He's never been one to take on lost causes. But maybe—just maybe—he's meant to help a hero find her way home.

Preface

Dear Reader,

Sometimes, a story gets lodged in your heart and refuses to be routed. *Jane's Long March Home* is one of those stories.

I was raised in a military family, so I suppose it's natural the Marine Corps would wind up as landscape in a lot of my writing. Working as a Labor and Delivery nurse, it was a short jaunt from there to penning stories about men and women with indomitable wills and their struggles to find home and family. That's how Jane was born—

In *Jane's Long March Home,* Gunnery Sergeant Jane Donovan made a mistake. She let a street urchin inside her defenses, and because she did, she's about to lose the one thing she values most, her life in the Corps.

Busy chasing a lucrative book deal that would legitimize his theories about treating war veterans suffering from Post Traumatic Stress Disorder, Chase Russell misses a client's cry for help. In the aftermath, he leaves his practice in Chicago to start over on a quiet, neglected Oregon ranch. When a cranky

Marine arrives on his doorstep, he wants nothing to do with the lady. But their attraction is irresistible.

What's an ex-counselor to do but make sure this hero finds her way home?

I hope you enjoy meeting Jane and Chase as much as I have enjoyed writing their story. You can contact me at my website: susanlute.com. I love to hear from readers.

OX! Susan

ONE

Hands under her armpits pulled Gunnery Sergeant Jane Donovan away from the hard surface mashing her face. Through a haze of alcohol, she heard her Corporal's voice among the sounds of the bar. "Come on, Gunny. It's time to hit the sack."

The disembodied words were filled with patience and something else. Pity. Jane swore. That was the last thing she wanted.

Easy anger flicked to life. The same anger she'd taken such pains to obliterate with the alcohol clogging her brain so she wouldn't remember.

Twisting away from the hands helping her into a nearby chair, she banged her fist on the table. Her vision cleared for a brief moment.

Corporal? She vigilantly searched her intoxicated memory. Yeah...Johnson.

"Johnson. I need a drink. Have a drink with me." She recognized the slurring, thick voice as her own, but just didn't give a damn. All that mattered was making the searing memories go away. "Come on…buy you a drink."

"No, Ma'am. I have orders to take you home and then escort you to a meeting with the CO at oh-seven-hundred."

Why couldn't they leave her alone? Anger pushed her beyond any oblivion the alcohol had provided. "Not going anywhere."

Lashing out, she aimed a fist at the Corporal's chin. It took a great deal of effort to bring the young Marine down to size. When he easily stepped out of reach, she overcompensated, twisting awkwardly, the mind-numbing stab to her hip a cruel reminder of why she was trying to drink herself into a stupor in the first place.

When the killer pain finally evaporated, she was lying on the NCO Club floor, staring at shined-to-perfection dress shoes.

"Okay. Let's get you home."

No fight left, she gave in to the hands lifting her, allowing the blackness nipping her heels to catch up.

Five hours later, Jane roused, flat on her back, staring at the bedroom ceiling as drums in her head synchronized with the pulsing throb of her miscreant hip. A battering sense of loss stirred up nausea in her stomach.

She'd been dreaming of that awful day again. The drum roll increased proportionately with the bitter anguish that never went away, no matter how often she drowned herself in booze.

Maybe, if she lay perfectly still, the piercing pain of her failure would disappear…for just one damn moment.

It didn't. The pounding in her head got louder.

"Gunnery Sergeant. It's oh-six-hundred."

Corporal Johnson. A vague memory of trying to knock the Corporal's lights out sent a wash of shame and regret over Jane, compounding the bleakness that was her constant companion.

"Go away, Johnson. That's an order." Her voice croaked dryly, evidence the amount of whiskey she'd consumed was not particularly compatible with human tissue or sanity.

The bedroom door cracked open. Johnson bravely stuck his head through the opening. "I have orders from the CO. You're to report to him at oh-seven-hundred."

Jane groaned, rolled onto her stomach, the better to block out the Corporal's baby face with his you're-my-superior-so-I-won't-sit-in-judgment-of-you expression. Well, the kid should pass judgment. She certainly judged herself guilty. She'd failed to do her duty. There was no way to go back and change that day now.

"Go make coffee. I don't need you to hold my hand while I shower."

"Yes, Ma'am."

Before the bedroom door closed, she called the young man back. "Johnson?"

"Yes, Ma'am?"

"I'm sorry about last night."

For the first time, the junior Marine smiled. "No problem, Ma'am. You didn't even come close."

Grimacing when the soft click hid the Corporal's cocky grin, she carefully maneuvered to a sitting position. The pounding in her head combined with the pain in her hip, as if competing in a wild disco dance contest. Her roiling stomach desperately attempted to keep up.

Battling her unstable gut, she dropped her aching head into shaking hands and took slow, deep breaths. *One step at a time,* she bleakly advised her battered body. That had been the best she could do since waking in a Turkish Military Hospital.

3

A cold shower and three strong, black coffees later, she was on her way to see her CO. Medication dulled the abuse from the night before and her body's response to the injuries that still hadn't completely healed. Sunglasses protected burning eyes from the sharp southern sun. Her watchdog, Corporal Johnson, acted as chauffeur.

Colonel Hawke motioned for them to enter. The lifer Marine was as lean and fierce as his name. A frown etched his sharp features, his pen tapping against the papers stacked in neat piles on the utilitarian desk.

"That will be all, Corporal."

"Yes, Sir." His expression stoic, Johnson quietly exited the austere room.

"I don't need a babysitter," she growled at the man who had been more of a mentor than a Commander over the last five years.

"I'll be the judge of that. Have a seat, Gunny."

Grateful for the respite offered her aching hip more than she was interested in obeying orders, Jane did as she was ordered. There wasn't much the Colonel could say that she hadn't already figured out for herself.

Hawke's scowl morphed into a frown. "When was the last time you had a decent meal?"

The night before all hell broke loose. She turned surly to hide the uneasiness joining the nausea in her stomach. "My eating habits aren't your problem, Sir."

"*You* are my problem, Gunny." Any softness in the Colonel's stern expression disappeared. He leaned on his arms, hands clasped on a file she presumed was hers. "You're a grenade ready to self-destruct. Drinking too much. Starting brawls in bars."

4

Putting steel in her spine, she pinned her gaze to the left of the Colonel's head. Through the window, summer sparkled, but she had no appreciation or appetite for the illusion of pastoral peace.

Filling her vision was a bomb strapped to a child's chest.

"Yes, Sir."

"That boy's death was not your fault. We have people who can help you deal with this."

"I don't need help, Sir." She'd spent uncountable months, first in a Turkish hospital, then, when her condition allowed traveling, at Bethesda Naval Hospital, talking to shrinks and counselors. Nobody had been able to "fix" the broken Marine.

The Colonel's tone took on a hard edge. "You've got new orders, Gunny."

Jane's scattered attention snapped back to Hawke's narrowed gaze. "Sir?"

"You're to report to Eagle's Outpost in Oregon for a special assignment. Your orders are to get well, physically and emotionally."

Uncontrolled anger slammed into Jane. For the first time in her military career, she considered disobeying a direct order.

Before she could mutiny, Colonel Hawke's uncompromising stare told her this assignment was not negotiable. "If you don't go, I will bust your ass right out of the Corps."

One week and one day later...

If this didn't work, the life she was so desperate to get back was headed down the toilet.

Jane parked her black Jeep next to an older white pickup. Well used and somewhat battered, it looked like she felt. Worn out and barely able to turn over her motor.

An unrelenting hammer pounded in her head, barely touched by the ibuprofen she'd swallowed earlier. Shoving a shaking hand through her unevenly cut hair, she bit back the bile threatening to crawl a burning path into her throat.

Okay, it was terror, but no one needed to know that but her. Focus Gunny.

She took in the house and the rundown, neglected buildings littering the yard around it. There was a long bunkhouse-like structure to one side. Beyond that, a huge barn and corrals that needed more than a little repair and paint.

A struggling lawn wrapped around the house. Juniper trees and an occasional tall pine grew on the hills behind the ranch house. Overhead, the sky was a clear blue. The air smelled clean. No... new and fresh, as if in this place, life had promise.

She had a hard time remembering the last time she'd felt that way. For a summer evening in early June, it was unseasonably warm in the Central Oregon high desert that bordered the Crooked River. That's what she'd heard on the radio as she navigated her way through the nearby town of Lone Pine.

She couldn't bring herself to care one way or the other. There wasn't anything she wouldn't give to not be here, but she was. For one thing and one thing only—to get the help she needed to resume the life that had been shattered by a terrorist bomb.

She used to be good at her job, at living a soldier's life. The best. She wasn't anymore. She'd made a holy mess of things, and the Colonel had given her one last chance to get her shit together.

Quelling the symptoms of being too long on the road without adequate food or sleep, she counted back the days.

ONE

Eight since she'd had any alcohol or a cigarette. Eight long days since the Colonel had given her his last ultimatum.

Get yourself squared away. If you don't, you can kiss your upcoming re-enlistment goodbye.

The words rang like a death knell in her ears. On this ranch, out in the middle of nowhere America, as far from the familiarity of a Marine base as it was possible to get, she'd been ordered to find what she'd lost. Somehow, she had to get her Marine *ooorah* back.

A movement by the long building caught her eye.

"Get out of the rig, Jane," she muttered, sweat slicking the palms of her hands where they gripped the steering wheel as if it were her last lifeline. "You're not going to save your ass by sitting here."

By sheer determination, she uncurled her fingers and climbed out of the Jeep. Squaring her shoulders, she cautiously approached the older man watching her. He pushed his cowboy hat to the back of his head, revealing short silver hair and bushy brows over canny, hazel eyes. Seams were cut into his weathered face from more than a few years spent under a hot sun.

"Can I help you, Miss?"

"I'm looking for Dr. Chase Russell."

"You have business with the Doc?"

Jane hesitated, then nodded. There was not an inch of give in the old man's expression. Fear stirred her nausea. He was going to tell her Russell wasn't here and send her away.

"You'll find the Doc out back, behind the house." The old codger pulled a rag from his pocket and swabbed at the back of his neck before turning to go inside the faded building.

"Thanks, Mr...?"

He glanced at her. "Gus'll do." And with that, he was gone.

Jane followed the grass around the house. Roses bloomed next to its side. Startlingly colorful petunias nestled beneath their thorny stems. Rounding the corner, she found a punching bag suspended from an ancient, gnarled apple tree. A man, hopefully, it was Russell, was giving it the old one-two punch.

He looked like he'd had plenty of practice. His muscled chest glistened with sweat. Workout pants hung indecently low on narrow hips. A growth of dark stubble shadowed a strong lower jaw.

Jane's stomach turned over, but this time not with the nerves she'd been fighting all morning. A twig snapped under her boot, causing him to look in her direction. Hair wet from hard exercise hung to his shoulders. Eyes the color of cinnamon checked her out, slowly making the trek from her face to her feet, taking in her black tank and the jeans tucked into her favorite lace-up boots.

When his gaze came back to her face, her skin flamed. The corners of his lips lifted into a welcoming smile. Her breath caught in her chest.

"I'm here to see Dr. Chase Russell," she stuttered.

Pulling off the boxing gloves, he hung them from the top of the bag before giving her his full attention. His sweats hung low, revealing the band of his briefs.

Jane jerked her gaze back to his face.

Remember why you're here.

He held out his hand. "That would be me."

Crap! "I'm Jane Donovan."

She put her hand in his. Awareness bolted up her arm.

"What can I do for you, Jane Donovan?"

Clearing her throat, she smartly gave him her military

8

identification. "Gunnery Sergeant Jane Donovan. Colonel Matthew Hawke sent me."

"My uncle?" That heart-stopping, flirtatious smile fled. "Why would he send you here?"

Stunned that he didn't know—surely the Colonel had told him. "He said you'd help me."

"With what?" Suspicion coating the words, Russell dropped her hand like a hot potato and stepped back. Not the welcome she'd expected.

Heat climbed into her face. "I'm having trouble sleeping. My conduct isn't...good." She added in a rush. "I don't care anymore."

It was more than she wanted to reveal, but that last part scared her more than anything. *Post Traumatic Stress Disorder.* She was beginning to hate the clinical designation.

A hint of understanding lit knowing eyes. Just as quickly, it disappeared. "I'm sorry. You've got the wrong guy."

"Dr. Chase Russell. I googled you. You're the author of *Strategies For The Country's New Walking Wounded.*" She hoped he didn't hear the desperation creeping into her voice.

He took another step away. "That doesn't mean I can help you."

"The Colonel said—" She had to get his cooperation. "He said you were a little unconventional but an expert in these matters." The information she'd uncovered on the internet confirmed the Colonel's assessment.

That drew a scowl from the man. "Wait here while I call my uncle."

All her life, Jane had worked hard to be on her best behavior, especially when she was a kid, hoping one of the nice couples who came to adopt one lucky child would pick her. Until she failed in Madrid, she'd succeeded.

The sight of the man she'd been told was her only salvation turning his back on her, pushed Jane to the verge of disobeying. Big time. Which was why she'd been sent to the ranch in the first place—to resolve her inability to hold it together.

That thought was all that kept her from immediately following Russell into the house. He'd better hurry because she didn't have the patience to wait long.

TWO

C hase hung up the phone, wondering how he was going to deal with the situation his uncle had thrust into his lap. He steeled himself against Matt's request, more an order, to let the Gunny stay.

He wanted, no, he required, solitude.

Though he'd told his uncle over and over he couldn't keep the Marine, it hadn't made a damn bit of difference. You-don't-run, you-stand-and-fight, Colonel Matthew Hawke, a many times decorated war hero, had one way and one way only to do things. That was charging straight through the middle. And right now, he wasn't happy his nephew had walked away from a successful Seattle practice to move to a remote Oregon ranch.

You can't run from what happened to Nate forever.

Chase pictured the woman he'd left outside. Remembered the potent awareness that kicked him in the gut the minute he'd laid eyes on her. He'd welcomed it. Frankly, considered the tug on his senses natural when clamping eyes on a beautiful lady. It was the first healthy reaction he'd had since Nate's hospitalization.

She'd stared back, cool blue eyes not missing a thing. Her full lips, so kissable, were an unsmiling slash across an angular, lean face. Blonde hair hung in chopped layers to her graceful neck. Of their own accord, his fingers itched to touch the silky strands.

Slender and tall, she exuded barely concealed, restless energy and wore an attitude like a boxer with a string of wins under her belt. With the sudden punch of desire to see how soft she was under that tough exterior, his pulse had lurched off the charts.

Chase didn't want to disappoint his uncle, but it was too late for that, wasn't it? He couldn't let his favorite relative use the sympathy building in his chest as leverage.

He was drained dry with nothing left to give. All he wanted was the sanctuary this lovely, neglected ranch had to offer.

Gunnery Sergeant Jane Donovan would not find what she was looking for here, and there was nothing he could…or was willing…to do about that.

When he turned to go tell the Marine she couldn't stay, there she was, just inside the kitchen door. Quick appreciation pricked him at the unconscious, proud angle of her sharply sculpted chin. So briefly, he almost missed it, a bruised little girl peeking out of the baby blues that stared him down.

She'd heard his side of the conversation. Chase swore under his breath. "I'm sorry you're caught in the middle here. I can give you the names of a couple of colleagues I trust."

Her chin angled higher. "The Colonel says you're the one, Sir. That you have experience dealing with my condition."

She took a shaky breath. A flicker of admiration that had

less to do with her stunning beauty and more with her courage sprang up in Chase's gut. She was braver than he was.

"This is important to me, Sir."

He had a sinking feeling it was going to take more than telling the Marine to leave to get her off his ranch. That left them on opposite sides, in an old-fashioned standoff.

He sighed in resignation. "I'm not your superior officer. Don't call me Sir."

~ * ~

Jane crossed her arms and hitched a hip against the door frame. Frustration rippled through her, but she wasn't about to tell the man refusing her request for help how close she was to having a full-blown panic attack. She'd had enough of them in the last six months to recognize the signs, and her future in the Corps depended on her staying calm and rational.

She shoved aside her fear. Jane knew what her problems were. She could list them as easily as any of the medical professionals she'd seen over the last six months. Insomnia. Nightmares when she did sleep. And fracturing memories that wouldn't fade. Trouble concentrating. Irritability that could flare into temper at the drop of a penny.

Their assessment? Not stable enough to be reassigned or to reenlist.

Something had to be done. She'd had no success at making the problems go away. Nor could she seem to hold it together so she could get through one day without breaking apart.

The only solution was to make the irritated man glaring at her understand how much she needed his 'special skills' to get her life back. Without resorting to begging, if possible. Not that she wouldn't do that, too, if it were necessary.

Perhaps a sneak attack through the back door would win him over. "You're not going to boot me out, are you?"

His scowl was not a good sign. "Is there any chance at all I can get you to leave?"

She took her time digging a piece of nicotine gum out of her front pocket and popped it out of its packaging and into her mouth. She glanced over her shoulder and shuddered.

"It'll be dark soon." It was in the dark when her worst ghosts came out to play.

Until Madrid, Jane had never been afraid of the dark. Not even at the orphanage where her drug-addicted mother had left her when she was four years old. In all the years she'd lived there, she'd welcomed the comfort of night.

After everyone went to sleep, she'd creep out of bed, find her way down shadowy halls to the dining room so she could snuggle in her favorite chair, and read the books Sister Mary Margaret kept for her there. When her eyes would no longer stay open, the nun would come along and send her to bed.

It was quite by accident that when she graduated from high school and enlisted in the Corps, she found the one thing she never expected to have—a family of her own. She couldn't lose that now, but how was she going to make Russell understand the dark was no longer her friend without sounding like a terrified little girl when she told him?

She settled for practicality instead. "It's a long way back to Parris Island, and I'm tired."

The scowl abruptly retreated from his handsome face. "You can stay the night. Use the first bedroom upstairs on your left."

Unspoken, she got his message loud and clear. *As soon as the sun rises, I want you out of here.* But for now, she had a bed for the night.

When he retreated to another part of the house, her bold front deserted her faster than air whooshing out of a deflating balloon. Chin dipping to her chest, her shoulders slumped. If he wouldn't help, where would that leave her? Where would she go?

Sister Mary Margaret wouldn't approve of giving up. Heading out the door she'd come in, Jane retraced her steps around the house to her Jeep. Grabbing the gear stashed there, she made her way to the room that had been assigned to her, vowing on the way to convince Russell—one way or another— to not only let her stay but, while he was at it, to fix what was broken inside.

~ * ~

In his office, desperate for the settled routine he'd managed to establish since coming to the ranch, Chase closed the computer file his uncle had sent on Gunny. The Marine's arrival had interrupted the unexciting routine of one day following the other, and he wanted it back.

The acid burning his gut suggested that wasn't in his immediate future. The sass in sky-blue eyes and the cocky arrogance in the nip of her hip against the door frame refused to be dislodged from his mind.

Gunnery Sergeant Jane Donovan challenged him in ways he didn't want to contemplate. So far, he'd managed to avoid examining too closely why he'd retreated to the ranch. His instinct for these things told him, letting her stay would force him to dig too deep into his own problems.

He had them. He just wanted to leave them in the past where

they belonged.

Restless, he went to the kitchen to warm up his coffee, then continued through to the dining room and sat at the table. Through the large picture window he'd put in to bring more light into the room, he found the Marine leaning against the weathered siding of the bunkhouse.

Leaving the counselor behind wasn't as easy as it should have been. And he was curious.

What had happened to take the light out of Jane Donovan's stunning eyes? According to the information Matt had sent, since the incident in Madrid, the Marine had turned into an absolute train wreck. Cited more times for drunk and disorderly conduct than he thought the Marine Corps had patience for, she'd also been to a long list of therapists who'd been unable to straighten her out.

Chase fought the awakening of professional interest he'd gone to a lot of trouble to lock away the night he walked out of his brother's hospital room. He would be crazy to let her stay. All she would do was disturb his new, quiet life.

He was a fraud. He knew it, and it was his family who'd suffered because of his bad judgment. It wasn't fair to put Jane at risk by pretending to be something he knew he wasn't.

The back door squeaked open, then slapped closed. Shortly, coffee in hand, his handyman joined him at the table.

Gus inclined his head in Jane's direction. "Who's the young lady?"

"A Marine passing through."

Gus's shaggy brows shot up. "She seems a bit lost."

In more ways than one, Chase couldn't help thinking, watching her curl and uncurl her fingers in a slow rhythm he knew was meant to soothe her. "She's leaving early tomorrow morning."

Pushing away from the building, she paced back and forth. A limp surfaced that he hadn't noticed earlier.

"She's been hurt." Concern colored the old man's quiet observation.

Chase frowned. From her file, he knew she'd been injured in the bombing, but there was no mention of it still giving her problems.

He kept his gaze locked on the woman fighting her demons in his yard. "Are you sticking around for dinner?"

He had a feeling he was going to need the buffer of the old gent between him and the Marine.

Gus shook his head. "Have a poker game in town."

"Will Maxine be there?" Chase hadn't met the woman, but it seemed something was going on between the lady who owned the next ranch over and his widowed handyman. Every week, Gus and his cronies met at the local bar to play cards. Most of the time, despite their protests, Maxine joined them.

A furrow formed between Gus's brows. "She's a stubborn woman who just won't listen to reason."

It seemed they had the same dilemma.

Gus pushed himself up from the table and clapped Chase on the back. "She's a pretty lass."

She most certainly was.

And that was the problem. As a woman, she had him thinking of warm summer nights, dinner over flickering candlelight that cast a golden glow on her tanned skin, and easy conversations while sipping champagne. Never once in these sudden imaginings was he sitting across from her, making notes in her medical record.

A twinge of self-reproach nicked Chase. He knew what it felt like not to know where to turn next. Jane Donovan deserved more from the person who would be her therapist than a has-been psychologist with nothing but lust on the brain.

After Gus left, he rose and stood at one side of the window, watching as she continued to pace out her agitation. Her jaw was clenched with stubborn resolve. And something else. Bruised honor? He knew a thing or two about that.

According to her file, she'd saved many lives that day in Madrid. The kid had been the only casualty. Why was she tearing her life down and throwing it away?

Chase shifted in irritation. It always started like this, with questions he shouldn't be asking if he had no intention of doing anything to find the answers.

He sucked in a breath, left the room, leaving the hurting Marine to her struggles. He didn't want to be interested in what those answers might be.

In the kitchen, he put two steaks on to broil. He would convince her to leave, even if it meant telling her the truth about his failure.

In the meantime, the least he could do was feed her. If that smacked of giving a condemned woman her last supper, he couldn't let that sway his decision.

THREE

Brooding over the wall she'd hit in the guise of the disturbing Dr. Chase Russell, Jane reminded herself he wasn't the enemy. That part was being played by her own mind.

She rubbed the ache in her hip and slowly crossed the yard to the house. Russell's ranch was a far cry from the orphanage she'd grown up in. When she was a kid, living in a place like this would have been a dream come true. It would have meant she'd been very good, indeed.

Part of her envied the man—that he had this serene place to sink his roots into. She'd only been there for a little over three hours, and for the first time since waking up in the Bethesda Hospital with a cranky hip and an even more cranky disposition, the sound of her heart pounding in her head had eased off to a dull thump.

Stopping just short of the wraparound porch, she stomped the dust from her boots. Out of habit, she patted her pockets, looking for a nonexistent pack of cigarettes. She dropped her hands, closed her eyes, and forced in a deep breath.

"I've got steaks grilling. Do you want a baked potato or rice?" Russell's deep baritone eased over her raw nerves, exciting a vision of long, barefoot walks on a South Carolina beach and of holding hands in the five o'clock hour before the stretch of warm sand filled with sunbathers. Her heartbeat stilled at the thought.

When she opened her eyes, he was studying her closely.

It was foolish to imagine scratching this unexpected itch. Doing something that reckless would only prove to Russell that everyone else was right—in her current undisciplined condition, she wasn't fit to go back to duty.

"Rice." Suddenly, she didn't want to stand idly by waiting for the other shoe to drop. "Is there something I can do to help?"

The man shrugged. "Sure. Do you cook?"

"Not so much, but I'm willing to give it a shot."

Strong brows shot straight up.

Jane winced. There were a lot of things she was good at—obeying orders, protecting her troops, developing good tactical plans. Cooking just didn't happen to be one of the skills in her arsenal. "Rice is easy, right?"

Russell's lips quirked into a brief half-smile. Jane was mesmerized. Quickly, she snatched herself free.

"All you have to do is follow the directions on the box."

She followed him inside. "That can't be too hard."

Surprisingly, it wasn't. When the meal was cooked and the table set, she dropped into a chair across from Russell, biting back a soft groan. It'd been a long drive from South Carolina. She was feeling every mile.

Her stiffening hip begged for relief, but first, she had to play nice. Sister Mary Margaret would approve of that tactic.

"Have you lived here long?"

Russell glanced up from cutting into his steak. "About three months."

Nerves had Jane reaching for anything that would keep the conversation with the taciturn man from descending into thick silence. "Where did you live before you came here?"

He hesitated. "Seattle."

"I've never been there."

The stern lines on his face eased. "It's a beautiful city."

The merry-go-round in Jane's stomach slowed. This wasn't so hard. "Why did you leave?"

"I needed a change." Russell's abrupt withdrawal ended their brief truce. His next question was proof enough. "What happened to your hip?"

He knew her story. She could tell. Despite her best efforts to hide it, he must have seen her limp. She bit her tongue to keep from lashing out, another new, bad habit.

Wiping all emotion from her voice, as calmly as she could manage, she gave him the skinny: "I was on the wrong end of a disagreement with a terrorist. The sciatic nerve is damaged."

"It didn't earn you a medical discharge?" His steady regard stirred things up in Jane's belly that she didn't want coming to life.

She shrugged, leaning her arms against the edge of the table. "The doctors say it'll get better. Looks like your place could use some work."

He nodded. "There are a few things that need to be done to get the ranch into shape."

In a valiant attempt to keep her disconcerting feelings contained, she picked up the fork and knife beside her plate and cut into the steak in front of her. "I could help."

"How?"

She flashed him the smile she'd learned early on could win her a favor or two. "I've been known to be handy with cleaning up an area."

Russell's eyes warmed to a clear brown that, unfortunately, was fast becoming Jane's favorite color.

It wasn't an invitation to stay, but he was listening. She took advantage of the opening. "I can paint. And, I'm good with small machines and engines."

He returned to his meal. "It's a nice offer, but I already have a handyman."

She shifted off her hip, confounded by his disinterest. This wasn't the same man she'd read about on the internet, the author of a book about soldiers with her condition.

Her mind covering the same old ground, she searched for leverage. "If it's a problem, I don't have to stay long. You can do your psychobabble thing, and I'll be gone in a week. Two tops."

Russell looked up from his plate, his face a blank slate. Surely, he could see how important this joint operation was.

He pointed at her plate with his knife. "Finish your dinner. Psychobabble, as you call it, isn't like taking a pill. You need a treatment plan. A week or two would only be enough time to get started. Besides the amount of time it would take to make any real progress on your problem, there's a very good reason why I can't be the one to help you, and my uncle knows that."

He scraped back his chair, carried his empty plate into the kitchen. Jane jumped up, feeling like a lost puppy attempting to get the nice man's attention, but she couldn't think of anything that would put the conversation back in the direction she desperately needed it to go.

Putting his dish in the dishwasher, without looking in her direction, Russell headed for the stairs. Frozen in disappointment, she watched him disappear upstairs.

Frantically searching for an argument she hadn't tried, anything that would bring him back and make him seriously reconsider her request, she blurted, "Wait, I—"

But it was too late. Outside the windows, dark settled like a suffocating pile of wool. Somewhere in the house, a clock chimed in the stillness, reminding her how much she'd grown to dislike the hours after midnight—each one too painfully intimate.

She barely held back from shoving her fist through the nearest wall. To keep her temper out of trouble, she finished cleaning the kitchen, not to win points, but because she was too disheartened to do anything else. To take her mind off the fact that once again she'd failed when so much was at stake, when she was done, she wandered from room to room.

She'd been to more counseling sessions than she could count, each time wishing she wasn't there. Many of her fellow Marines had been involved in worse incidents than she had and been able to keep it together, do their duty, and move on to the next assignment.

It was demoralizing. What was wrong with her? Jane battled the discouragement crushing her. Russell was the last train stop on the road to her guillotine.

For a moment, she'd thought she had a chance to wipe her slate clean, get back the courage she'd lost. There was something in the man's face when he looked at her. Something was hiding beneath his resentment at having her show up out of the blue. An indefinable glimmer, as if somehow he seemed to understand where she'd been, what had happened to change her from that good girl Sister Mary Margaret had been proud of, to someone who wasn't so good anymore.

But it'd turned out to be a dead end. Coming to a halt just inside a room that still bore the odor of fresh paint, Jane sneered at her naivete.

She was a Marine. *Ooorah.* Marines didn't give up. It looked like the time to beg had come.

She turned slowly. A couch and two chairs lounged around a heavy square coffee table, facing a large fireplace. Bookshelves leaned against the wall next to her.

There was no television or computer in the room, which seemed odd. Russell struck her as a Saturday sports kind of guy. Decked out in earth tones, the only other color in the room was a tall stack of books on the floor next to one of the chairs.

Except for the stack, the room had a silent air that said a lot about the man. In other circumstances, Jane might have been interested in finding out why he didn't spend enough time in the appealing room to even leave a discarded glass or piece of mail.

If this were her home, with its quiet, tranquilizing feel, this room would be her favorite. It was a place where troubles wouldn't intrude, and secret dreams would dare to come out of the dark where they were hiding.

She flipped back the cover of the top book, *Treatment Strategies For The Country's New Walking Wounded*, by Dr. Chase Russell. His book.

She snatched it up. The cover fell open to the dedication page.

This book has been a labor of love and is dedicated to my family— my Mom and Dad, Elaine and Mike Russell, and my brother Nate.

You're my bedrock.

Jane's anxiety slipped unguarded into temper. She flipped to the index. The man was a freaking expert in the field of treating military personnel returning from war with symptoms of post-traumatic—

The book abruptly flew from her hands.

She whirled to face Russell. His face impassive, he put the tome out of reach on the bookshelf.

"Hey."

"That's not very interesting reading. I have a Tom Clancy in that stack you might prefer."

Her temper tied Jane up. She didn't understand. If he was so clever at treating soldiers with her problems, why did he live on a rundown ranch in more need of repair than she was? More importantly, why was he so determined not to help her?

Holding onto her tumbling emotions, she locked her jaws until they ached. If she wanted answers, staying in control—a challenge at the best of times—was her only recourse.

"I'm a huge fan of Anne McCaffrey and Katie MacAlister."

His eyes never left her face. Attacked by a sudden awareness she didn't want, she glanced around the room, her gaze lighting on a photograph on the mantle.

Space. She needed some space before she said the hell with it, grabbed his shirt, and dragged him close to discover if he tasted as good as he looked.

She edged away to study the photo closely.

Whoever had taken the picture had captured two young men, one of them Russell, looking much younger. He was clowning around, his arm locked around the neck of the other one, free hand curled in a fist, playfully aimed at his smiling hostage's stomach.

The grin reached the younger Russell's eyes. How had the lighthearted, laughing guy in the picture become the withdrawn, resigned man behind her? Maybe the answer lay in the dedication in his book. "Nate?"

He nodded.

Filing the information for later, she moved on to the only other adornment in the room. Two ink and pencil drawings hung on either side of the fireplace. In the drawings, two young children bearing a remarkable resemblance to the young men in the photograph played in a park.

She raised one brow in Russell's direction. The hard lines around his mouth softened. "My mother drew them. When we were kids, after school, we'd go to the bookstore she and my dad owned to do our homework. Sometimes we'd look up and there she'd be with her sketch pad."

At the wistful look on his face, Jane went still. The back door she was looking for creaked open, but Russell didn't let her linger there.

As quick as he'd opened up, he changed back into the perfect host. Aloof and all business. "There's a television in your room. I left a heating pad on the bed."

Her patience, what little she had left, snapped.

"I don't get what your problem is. You have to be at the top of your game to get a book like that published." She waved a frustrated hand at the book he'd taken. Like a full-blown hurricane, her turbulent emotions broke free of her fraying restraint. "So, is this the end of the road for me? What am I supposed to do? Lay down my gun and surrender?"

Russell moved fast, so fast Jane didn't see him coming. His large hands dug into her shoulders, his eyes losing that yummy shade of brown she'd come to expect. "This is the end of the road only if you want it to be. Don't ever give up!"

Caught by surprise, she put a hand against his chest and pushed hard. She could feel the heat of his body through the cotton shirt. The accelerated thump of his heart captured the unwanted girl that still resided in Jane.

Which was crazy. No man had ever reached that deep inside her. "I don't want to, but if you won't help me–"

She left the sentence unfinished.

He forced out a breath. "It's not you. It's me. I'm not what you need."

"What I need?" Jane didn't like the sound of that. Not once since she'd accepted she wasn't the kind of kid prospective parents lined up to adopt had she needed anything or anybody. That's what made it that much harder to admit her failure to Russell. "I thought I could do this on my own. Get better. But I can't. Everything's wrong. I can't hold it together."

"Nightmares?"

The strength of his frowning stare gave her courage. She allowed one shaky jerk of her chin.

The hands on her shoulders dropped. A sigh escaped his chest. "I had a very successful practice in Seattle, treating soldiers with problems—"

"—like mine."

Russell nodded. "One of them was Nate."

"Your brother?"

All emotion stripped away, he stiffly recited as if reading from a case file, "One night, I was hosting a party to celebrate the success of my recently published book."

His lip curled derisively. "There I was, having a grand old time. Local booksellers came, and a book reviewer from the Seattle Tribune. My agent and editor had flown in to discuss an interview request from a national television station."

He paused. Jane leaned against the cold fireplace. So far, she couldn't see a downside or what had made Russell drop everything and start over so far away from his family. If what he was saying was true, he should be proud of what he'd accomplished.

"I turned off my cell that night and ignored, missed, whatever you want to call it, it doesn't matter, the call from my brother. After the party was over, Mom finally got through. She and Dad had taken Nate to the hospital for a drug overdose."

Jane's shoulders stiffened as she watched her hopes for Russell's help go down the drain.

"After that, I couldn't do it anymore. I couldn't be responsible for saving fractured lives. So, I bought this ranch and walked away. I can't trust myself, and you sure as hell shouldn't, either."

The stubbornness that had gotten her this far straightened her spine. "You just told me not to give up. Are you only good at giving advice?"

His burning gaze narrowed on her. "You shouldn't have to settle for a therapist who's made such a mess of his own life."

Silence stretched between them as Russell waited for her judgment, but Jane didn't have any to give him. How could she condemn his actions when hers had almost resulted in the death of a whole compound of people? She was at least responsible for the death of the homeless boy she'd taken under her wing.

Linus shouldn't have died. If she'd only been quicker, talked faster, she could have extracted him from the bomb that had been meant to take out the embassy.

So, they had the worst kind of failure in common. She could see it in the self-condemnation etched into the sharp planes of his face. It wasn't enough to make her back off.

So she fought for the life she wanted back. "I'm sorry about your brother. I have a feeling that if it were me telling you that story, you'd say something like, *Life happens. There's nothing you can do but move on.*"

Russell's lips twitched. She couldn't keep the corners of her own lips from shifting in response.

"You're pretty good at this. Are you sure you're the one who needs counseling?"

"So they tell me." Dispirited, Jane backed into the hall. "I'll pack my gear and be out of your hair first thing in the morning."

Later, flipping to his back in a futile effort to find the sleep eluding him, Chase attempted to erase from his overactive mind the look of defeat on Jane's face when she'd finally accepted he couldn't help her.

When he heard the creak of her bed, followed by the sound of channel surfing, he stared at the ceiling lit by the moon from the window. Jane Donovan had more spunk and courage than any woman he'd ever met. It would not be smart to change his decision.

He turned onto his side, finally drifting off to sleep with the image of the Marine front and center in his mind, all starch and vinegar on the outside, vulnerable pride on the inside.

His dreams morphed as he slipped into a cold hospital room, where he used every argument he could to talk his little brother into putting the bottle of pills down.

It wasn't until later, when he was startled awake, drenched in a chilling sweat, that he realized Nate's face had morphed into Jane's wounded blue eyes, and it was she who called out to him, a desperation in her trembling voice he could no longer ignore.

FOUR

The next morning, Chase had to see for himself that Jane was okay. Hearing the low sound of the television, he knocked softly on her bedroom door. When there was no response, and with his nightmare still fresh in his mind, he inched into the room.

The sight that met his eyes had his pulse taking off like a rocket. The sheet, barely covering her essentials, slipped even more as the Marine shifted restlessly in her sleep. Her blonde hair stuck out in long spikes on the pillow. His stomach flipped over in a sudden hunger that had nothing to do with a desire for breakfast.

As quietly as he'd opened the door, he closed it. The last thing he needed was to think of Jane Donovan as anything other than a client. He sighed, resigned because sometime in the night, he'd decided to work with her.

He'd have to keep a professional distance, something he'd been unable to do with Nate, but he didn't kid himself. It wouldn't be easy.

Everything he'd been taught said he shouldn't have been treating a family member, but his brother had refused to see anyone else. Caught between his professionalism and his love for Nate, Chase hadn't been able to turn his back on a soldier's suffering then, either.

This time, he couldn't assume he had all the answers. He couldn't look at Jane as anything other than a patient. Someone who needed his expertise. Even if the vulnerability she covered with that tough-as-nails Marine armor made him want to scoop her up and do more than simply console her.

When she wasn't down for breakfast by the time he was finished, he left a short stack of pancakes in the microwave and a note instructing her to come to the bunkhouse when she'd eaten.

It was disconcerting to discover he wanted to make sure the Marine got three square meals a day; that all he could think about was how to make the challenge of facing her fears easier; that he was hoping to draw another one of those tiny smiles out of her.

At the bunkhouse, while he waited for Jane to surface, Chase considered her treatment plan as he swept debris into a pile in the middle of the floor.

When he'd had his practice, he'd earned a reputation for being ruthless when it came to getting results from the not-always-compliant walking wounded. His uncle knew that, which was why he'd sent his Marine across the country and placed her in his care.

Well, Matt had gotten his wish. When they were done, he'd send her back to active duty with the skills she needed to see her through the hard times. Living and moving beyond the tragedy still wouldn't be easy, but she'd have a running start.

At the thought, there would come a time when he wouldn't be around to help her through those new challenges, a surprising, uncomfortable clink sounded against the wall he'd erected so he could be her counselor.

"I'm ready to leave."

Chase glanced up at the woman so completely taking over his thoughts. She stood in the doorway he'd left open.

Birds chirped in the yard behind her. Dust particles settled between them. The clean scent of her recent shower assailed him. Backlit by morning sunlight, she looked like an angel.

Just stick to the plan, Russell.

Clearing his throat, he leaned on the broom. "I've decided to help you."

"Why?" A furrow formed between her exquisite brows.

She should be happy with his decision, but Chase couldn't see what emotions, or lack of them, might have sprung into shrewd blue eyes hidden by the aviator glasses favored by military personnel.

"You were right. I could use an extra pair of hands to help get things squared away here."

"Begging your pardon, Dr. Russell."

Chase held up one hand. Should he tell her the truth? She certainly deserved it after everything she'd been through.

That night at his brother's hospital bedside, it'd been humbling to discover he wasn't such a big shot after all. What if Matt was right, and this Marine was his one chance to right his grievous mistake?

He released his breath with a harsh hiss and admitted, "If I work with you, it will help me, too."

Jane stared, clearly confused by his change of heart.

"What do you say? Will you stay?"

Removing her sunglasses, she hung them on the neck of her tank top. Pulling gum from her jeans pocket, she didn't do a good job of hiding her belligerence. "I have nowhere else to be."

Chase had a hard time hiding his smile. "How long can you stay?"

"I've got thirty days' leave coming."

He considered how much they had to do. Thirty days wasn't much time, but accepting the constraint, he sought her gaze beneath the tinted glasses. "There will be ground rules."

For the briefest moment, he thought he saw relief flit across the face that had him thinking she was a woman used to taking care of herself. "Yes, Sir."

Forbidding his gaze to flick down her thin, athletic frame, he laid them out. "First, you've got to stop calling me Sir. Second, you'll eat three meals a day."

"I eat enough."

He ignored her. "I'll organize daily therapy sessions."

"Talking." She sounded dubious. Chase opted to tell her later that there was more.

"What do you do for exercise?"

Her brows shot up.

She was a Marine in his uncle's command. Chase knew what that meant. He hadn't forgotten the summers he and Nate had spent with Matt backpacking into the rugged Central Oregon countryside, rock climbing at nearby Smith Rock, and white water rafting on the Deschutes River.

Matt had expected them to stay in top physical condition. He wouldn't demand anything less from his Marines.

Those adolescent memories were primarily what had drawn Chase to the area. When he'd come across the For Sale sign out on the road fronting the ranch on his last vacation, he'd bought the place thinking it would be a great vacation home. Little did he know it would become his sanctuary.

"Okay, we'll work out an exercise program later." For the first time since taking up residence, Chase relaxed. Jane Donovan was not going to make the next month easy. The only surprise was, he kind of liked that about her. "You'll need to learn some relaxation techniques."

"I'm relaxed."

"Uh-huh. I can see that." His comment brought out a sexy scowl that stirred his gut in appreciation. "There are enough chores to do around here to keep you from brooding."

Her scowl deepened. "I don't brood."

"In between all that, we'll go over your coping mechanisms."

"I won't take pills."

"All right, can you tell me why?"

She blushed prettily, then squared her shoulders. "They take my will away. You should also know that alcohol doesn't help."

"Glad to hear that." There had been a note about excessive alcohol use in her file.

"I hope you have some new tricks up your sleeve because *talking* about *how I'm feeling* doesn't help either."

The woman was as dangerous as dynamite. One more time, he warned himself to keep his mind on the game and not on how interesting she was becoming.

Before he could forget he was a professional, he pointed over her shoulder. "Change into workout clothes and meet me out back at the punching bag."

Fifteen minutes later, Jane had her gear stowed in the room where she'd slept the night through for the first time since the bombing. A heavy dose of ibuprofen and the heating pad

Russell had left on the bed had given her the reprieve she'd all but given up finding.

When she got down to the punching bag, she wasn't as relieved as she thought she would be to find her new counselor waiting.

She could do this. She'd had too many therapists over the last six months not to know what Russell wanted to hear. Like he said, there wasn't much time. All she had to do was give him the right answers. He would work his magic. She'd be on her way home.

He handed her a pair of fat, padded boxing gloves. "Do you know how to box?"

"I've had some practice." In Madrid, besides Friday night poker, it had been one of their favorite pastimes.

Russell pulled on matching gloves. He moved to the opposite side of the bag and threw a punch that landed with a hard thud. "So, you were raised in an orphanage? Did you know your family?"

The counselor didn't waste any time. Jane danced in to throw a punch, not answering for a long string of heartbeats. She didn't like talking about her mother. But Russell wanted to talk. It was going to be a very short conversation.

"My mother died of an overdose a few years after she left me with the nuns at St. Mary's."

She retreated on the balls of her feet, feeling a pinch in her right leg that matched the one in her heart. She swore under her breath, then came back, delivering a swift one-two to the bag.

"I'm sorry." He was silent, his look thoughtful, making her edgier than she already felt. "What was it like, growing up there?"

Breathing hard, she took a sideways step, inching around the perimeter of the bag. Russell kept pace with her.

She glanced at him and smirked. "I had a particular talent with a Slim Jim."

"Sounds like a tough life."

"Sister Mary Margaret did the best she could with what she had to work with." She gave the bag several more punishing blows, making it rotate back and forth. "Should I be lying on a couch or something, Dr. Russell?"

He made her pay for the sarcasm she wouldn't keep in check by taking the conversation to a place she didn't want to go. "How's your hip holding up?"

"Fine."

Constant discomfort was a reminder of how she'd failed to do her duty. She attached the bag with a ferocious sequence of hits that rocked it toward Russell. He bared his teeth in a smile that harbored devastating understanding.

Not wanting his pity, she clenched her jaw tight enough to ache along with her hip. All she wanted from the Doc was for him to hand her life back in one piece.

"Tell me about Sister Mary Margaret."

Her growl was surly, even to her own ears. "What does she have to do with anything?"

"If you want to go back to work—" His implication was clear. Jane chomped on her gum. She'd gnawed every bit of nicotine out of it and wished she'd brought more down with her. Dancing another step around the bag, the force of her next strike reverberated up her arm, settling her as nothing else had so far.

"There's not much to tell."

"Tell me about the orphanage, then. Do you ever go back?"

"There's nothing to go back for." *Except Sister Mary Margaret.* The one person who'd believed in her.

It'd been too long since Jane had last seen the nun, but she hadn't wanted the lady who'd had such a huge impact on her life to see how far down the rabbit hole she'd fallen.

She stepped back and, taking several deep breaths, planted her gloved hands on her hips.

Russell's hits were getting too close. She *would* cooperate with him—tell him what he wanted to know. But for now, she needed a little breathing room. "Look, I've heard it all before. What happened in Madrid wasn't my fault. I couldn't have prevented the bombing. I was in the wrong place at the wrong time."

Each time she'd heard the words, and she'd heard them often enough, a bile of grief pushed into her throat, making it almost impossible to breathe. All those therapists had wanted her to believe that bull, but no matter how hard she tried—

A shrewdness she hadn't expected from the man sparing with her muted the sting of his next words. "You don't believe it. If you did, you wouldn't be here needing my help."

She stared at her feet, holding herself perfectly still while silently counting to ten. Stiffly, she conceded. Anything to give him the ammunition he needed to rout her demons.

"Of course, you're right."

But Russell wanted more. "Talk to me, Gunny." An order, not a request.

Goaded, she spat, "Madrid had nothing to do with my Marine training." The truth of that startled her.

"What do you mean?"

Drowning in the sudden realization that it was growing up an orphan that had betrayed her, she scowled fiercely and, willing her feet to stay put, shouted, "I don't know."

"Okay. Let's try another tack."

Suspicion erupted like a shot from a scattergun. Keeping up with the Doc was turning into a full-time job. But she'd asked for his help, and just because he'd touched a sore spot, it sure as hell didn't mean she would let him push her into retreat this early in the game.

"Has any of your therapists tried Play Therapy with you?"

"Play therapy." She pulled off her gloves.

"Originally, it was developed to help children recover from psychological trauma." He eyed her with a good dose of speculation. Jane squirmed. What was the hunky therapist up to now? "I've had some success using this modality on adults. I like it because it's a safe, non-threatening way to explore feelings we might not be able to untangle, in a reasonable amount of time, using a more conventional method."

"English, Doc." Jane dropped her gloves and grabbed one of the water bottles from the edge of the porch.

"It'll work."

His assurance didn't settle the battle being fought in her stomach. Play like a kid? She was willing to give anything a try. "Whatever. You're the Doc."

His gloves hit the dirt. "What kind of games did you play at the orphanage?"

"I mentioned the Slim Jim, right?"

He grabbed up the remaining bottle and uncapped it. "Before that. Board games? Playing in a sandbox? Hide and seek?"

Fascinated, Jane watched his throat work as he gulped down the water, waiting for her answer.

What would it be like to be the one lapping the moisture from his lips? More than a little distracted, she scrambled to remember his question.

Games. When she was a kid. That was it.

"Um… jump rope. Dodgeball. And I ran track in middle school."

His gaze slid down her body to her hip. Heat flared across her skin, and not because the day was turning into a hot one. "I was thinking of something a little tamer. Have you ever played hopscotch?"

"I don't think so." She'd watched the younger kids hop the connected blocks but never joined in herself.

His brows raised in surprise. "Well, we're going to change that right now."

He led her to a hard-packed patch of dirt.

Hopscotch? Was the child's game some kind of bizarre therapy?

Besieged by an attack of attraction for the man she was counting on to give her life back, Jane couldn't take her eyes off the display of strong muscles as he drew a string of linked squares on the ground.

He handed her one of the two flat stones he found nearby. "Do you know how to play?"

She swallowed back the lump making it difficult to breathe. She wasn't about to blow her last chance to get her life back just because she had the hots for her therapist. Anyway, it was just lust, right?

"You go first."

Amusement warmed the color of his eyes and turned her resolve to keep her distance to mush.

He tossed his stone into the first square. "Did you like Spain?"

He hopped over the stone into the next square and continued

along the hopscotch, hopping on one foot, landing with a foot in each set of side-by-side squares, until he reached the end. He flipped around.

The look of utter enjoyment on his face was priceless. An unaccustomed pressure built in her chest. A grown man voluntarily playing a child's game moved something there she didn't know was lurking.

What woman wouldn't want a man who had the looks of a Mount Olympus god and who could also play like a child to help a wounded soldier?

"It wasn't home, but I liked it."

He started back. "Did you leave anyone there? Friends? Someone who cares what happens to you?"

"No." The answer shot out of her.

After the incident in Madrid, after losing Linus, she'd dropped contact with her buddies at the embassy. Another strike against her.

She knew better than to shut them down the way she had. At first, she just didn't give a damn about staying in touch, pretending she hadn't made the biggest mistake of her career.

Then, she didn't know how to apologize for her behavior. It was totally out of line. If she'd been in their place, she certainly wouldn't have put up with it.

Russell leaned over to pick up his stone, then cast her a smug glance, as though he could see the rage and anxiety swirling in her belly. "Your turn."

She tossed her stone, barely keeping it inside the square, then hopped over it, and determined to complete this one simple task, wiped everything else from her mind. Following Russell's example, she made it to the far end of the hopscotch, took a small jump, and twisted to return the way she'd come.

Sharp pain stabbed her hip. Her vision blurred, and suddenly, there she was, in the basement of the embassy, facing the boy she'd befriended. Linus's eyes were dark with the brainwashing drugs terrorists had pumped into him. Suffocating. Terrifying. A homemade bomb was strapped to his chest.

She had no excuse for not figuring out that as an orphan, the boy could be approached and used as a pawn by terrorists who would use even children to get to their target.

She'd thought she was making his life better. Now, because of his association with her, the kid had no life at all.

"Jane—" Fingers digging into her shoulder brought her back to the present. Russell hovered too close, concern drawing his brows together. "Are you okay?"

She shook her head. The image always came without warning, and when she least expected it. She knew there was more, but it was all she remembered of that last moment before a loud explosion brought the building down on top of her.

Bitterness spilled over, threatening her hard-won equilibrium. Her heart pounded, torn in two, burning with the pain of a loss that shouldn't have happened that way.

Sweat beading her upper lip, Jane backed up from the memory. All she could think of was finding the nearest bar. She shrugged off Russell's immobilizing grip. "I'm done playing."

He blocked her escape. "Okay, we're moving too fast. No problem."

She gulped in several rapid breaths to slow the thumping in her ears. Her swimming gaze snapped up to Russell's. The concern he didn't bother to hide caused a silly flip-flop in the region of her heart. The way his lips curled up on the edges was

a killer. She was too slow, slamming her defenses up against
it.

The struggling breath in her chest stilled. What *would* it feel
like to press her lips to his? To see if he could move her beyond
this cold inner landscape she'd lingered in too long?

Then the craziness of it slapped her. The truth was, thinking
about kissing the daylights out of her therapist was a nice
distraction, but it wasn't part of her mission, and it wouldn't
get her home any faster.

She wanted his help, but doing as he asked, remembering
was just too damn painful.

A loud crash from inside the house broke the tension
spinning between them. A boy's scared face appeared at the
screened back door, and all of a sudden, how much she was
attracted to the Doc was the least of Jane's worries.

FIVE

The boy disappeared. Russell sprinted into the house. Instantly thrown into military mode, Jane slipped around to the front to cut off the kid's escape. Focused on getting away, he didn't see her until it was too late.

As quick as a striking snake, she nabbed him by the back of the neck. Apples and energy bars were scattered onto the ground.

"What have we here?" When he tried to jerk free, she tightened her grip. "Settle down. You're not going anywhere, kid."

She looked him over. He was about an inch shorter than her own five feet nine. Probably thirteen or fourteen. He had unkempt dark brown hair and wild eyes.

Another face was superimposed over his. *Linus.* Unable to easily pronounce his real name, she'd called him that after the Peanuts character he'd reminded her of.

Sensing her sudden weakness, the boy she was hanging on

to struggled against her firm grip.

"Be still," she growled, giving him a shake to let him know she was dead serious.

Emerging from the house, Russell took hold of the kid's arm. A faint cry came from the direction of the barn. Gus stuck his head out. "Got a kid down in here."

The boy lashed out with his feet and won his freedom to race ahead to the barn, shouting, "Leave my brother alone."

Admiring his nerve, Jane reluctantly followed Russell.

She should be grateful for the distracted interest that filtered across the Doc's handsome face. It meant he wasn't lingering on that little episode, aborting his *play* therapy.

At the end, something had passed between them. Not sympathy. Or pity. A promise, perhaps that he wouldn't give up on her, no matter how much bull she threw at him. Which could be a lot, given her present state of mind.

She slipped into the barn, stopping just inside to adjust to the dim interior. Russell and Gus squatted next to a small child— he couldn't have been more than five or six—lying motionless on the hay-covered floor. The teen she'd caught stood over them, fear-laden eyes darting from face to face with equal parts anger and apprehension.

A quick assessment had Jane locking up her seriously stormy emotions. She would wager a king's ransom these kids were homeless, runaways maybe, but definitely without a loving family to look after them. She knew the signs.

One look at Russell's face, the concern pulling at the edges of his mouth, and she was swearing under her breath. There wasn't a doubt in her mind he was about to offer the children sanctuary; in fact, would insist on making whatever was wrong, right for them.

What man with his background wouldn't? Worse than that? Jane knew if it was left up to her, she would do the same thing. Despite whatever mistakes she'd made in Madrid, she would do whatever it took to help these kids, too.

The revelation was a shock, but it didn't change things. Mentally, she did what no Marine did. She retreated.

What happens to these kids has nothing to do with you.

"I'm okay."

"He's not hurt." Alarm made the boys' voices squeak.

"We need to see how badly he's injured," Russell spoke directly to the older boy, his tone discouraging any argument.

Jane wiped her sweaty palms on her pants.

The teenager's lips compressed together in a belligerent slash across his none-too-clean face. She knew that look. The memory had a face. It slammed her in the gut.

Wanting more than anything to leave the suffocating, cavernous barn, she started to back up. As much to distance herself from the sight of Russell murmuring encouragement as he calmly checked the frightened boy for injuries, as from an overwhelming need to protect herself from the panic spilling from the dark eyes of the older kid.

"I could use some help here." Russell's sudden, steady regard halted her hasty retreat while daring her to cross over the line into his camp. She knew what Sister Mary Margaret would expect her to do.

The little guy attempted to sit up. Straw clung to his clothes.

From a distance, reluctant to give up, Jane offered, "It'd probably be best to keep him still until you're sure he's not injured."

"Good advice. Thanks," Russell sneered. Placing a firm hand on the kid's shoulder to hold him still, he shot her an exasperated look that almost had her smiling. Almost.

She sighed heavily. A good Marine always obeyed orders, she reminded herself, dropping to her knees at the boy's feet. Starting at his thighs, she checked for fractures, working her way toward his well-worn sneakers.

"Leave him alone!"

"We won't hurt him." Russell's reassurance was just a shade too welcome. Her edginess dissipated like a squall suddenly gone to the ground. The older boy hovering over them shoved his hands in his pockets and stood down, too.

The Doc certainly had a way with casualties. That shouldn't be so surprising, she decided, locking her attention on the teenager. "What's your name, kid?"

Instead of answering, he braced his feet on the straw-littered floor. Cocky, scared, and too easy to read, he smelled of trouble with a capital T.

Jane had been where he was, had done far worse than steal a few apples when she was his age. Unwanted sympathy shimmied beneath the barricade she'd built around her heart.

"Tell the lady your name," Russell ordered softly.

"Bobby…uh Bobby Jones."

Not his real name. She could guarantee it. Jane knew all the games of survival. Why didn't Russell just call 911 and the authorities and be done with them?

He caught her eye, reading her thoughts. Silently, he taunted her to become his co-conspirator. She held back in self-preservation, unwilling to be dragged into whatever maneuvers the man had planned.

Russell broke eye contact, resuming his interrogation. "So, why are you boys stealing food?"

Gus shuffled his feet, grumbling his verdict in the absence

of a response from Bobby. "Hooligans, that's why they were stealing."

Jane sighed. A "special gift", the nuns had called her ability to calm the new arrivals at the orphanage. It was the *gift* that had betrayed her.

It wasn't smart to lend Russell a hand with the boys, but she couldn't stop herself. Surrendering to her fate, she set her sights on the one she figured would be the most likely to spill his guts. "My name's Jane. What's yours?"

The injured boy looked at his big brother. Bobby nodded in a spare movement as if anything they did could reveal who they were and what they were doing there.

The little guy shifted his tired gaze to Jane. "Pete. Ow!"

Her heart taking a hit, she removed her hands from his foot. "His ankle's probably broken. He'll need X-rays to be sure."

"We're not going to the hospital."

"You have no choice. There's nothing here on the ranch that will help us determine how badly your brother is injured." Discouraging further discussion, Russell picked up Pete. "Jane, you ride in the backseat with Pete to keep his ankle stabilized."

Oh no, that's not going to happen. She raised a brow. "It'd be better if I stayed here."

She'd agreed to cooperate fully with Russell, but no way was she going to reveal this early in the game that the Marine he'd decided to let stay on his ranch had more than a few skeletons of her own. One of them, an unreasonable fear of hospitals.

He cast her a sharp look. "Move it, Marine."

Jane swore under her breath. The man saw way too much.

Leaning on years of long, hard training, she pulled herself together, focusing on the children's distress. Apprehension danced on their faces, matching the emotions churning up acid in her stomach.

"Yes, Sir," she spat, putting the sharp snap of a silent salute into the words.

Russell's lips twitched. Unexpectedly, she felt better.

He carried Pete to the older model crew cab F150. Wearing a mulish look, Bobby followed close behind. "I'm going with you."

"Figured you would," Russell tossed over his shoulder, luring Jane further into his trap.

Little Pete kept his frantic gaze locked on his brother, silently begging Bobby to extract him from the clutches of these strangers. That's when Jane's defenses buckled. First, by Russell's compassionate handling of the boys. Where had that come from? And then, by the obvious bond between the two brothers.

The closest thing she'd ever had to having a brother was her fellow soldiers in the Corps. Before she could do anything more to stop him, Russell had her loaded in the backseat, cradling Pete's ankle in her lap. Bobby called shotgun.

In the tense silence that rode with them, the Doc carefully negotiated the long drive that headed toward the nearest Emergency Room. It didn't get past Jane that his ride was the same color as a white knight's steed. Wasn't it good that she didn't believe in silly fairy tales?

His eyes met hers in the rear-view mirror, then crinkled at the outer corners in approval. Jane's breath stalled. A flush of pure awareness heated her skin.

How the Sam Hill had she ended up here?

Saving your career, that's how.

Pete winced as they hit an uneven patch of road. Tearing away from the image of Russell doing more than offering an approval she neither wanted nor needed, she repositioned her hands to give the boy's leg more stability.

~ * ~

Chase was more than ready to transport his recalcitrant group back to the ranch. It was past one in the morning, and he was tired and not in a good mood.

An X-ray of Pete's leg had uncovered a hairline fracture, making a short cast necessary. Five hours after their arrival, the antiseptic smell of the emergency department was too much, as was the brooding silence that greeted his attempts to elicit any useful information from his uninvited guests.

His head hurt at finding himself responsible for a soldier's mental and physical well-being. And now, these kids, too? That last was easily solved when he turned Bobby and Pete over to child services. His friend, Beth, would know what to do with them.

He'd come to Oregon seeking refuge. Along the way, he'd hoped to find his truth, whatever that might be. Deciding to take Jane on was one thing. Thinking about adding two runaway kids to the mix was another.

Still, he was considering it.

Chase massaged the back of his neck. He'd have to decide what to do about the boys after getting whatever sleep could be wrestled from the rest of the night.

He caught sight of the Marine pacing outside the glass doors on his way to pay the bill. The poor woman hadn't stepped one foot into the hospital since their arrival. Unfortunately, the fact that she was now his client, and persona non grata because of it, didn't stop the attraction sneaking up on him or keep him from wondering who she was under all that spit and polish.

She wouldn't appreciate his dubious interest. And after her emotional tumble during their game of hopscotch, he shouldn't be thinking it, but there it was.

Put a cork in it, Russell. He sighed heavily. Easier said than done.

"Sign here, please." The young woman on the other side of the spotless counter handed him back his credit card, along with a receipt to sign. Disturbed by how his life was getting cluttered up, he signed where she indicated, unable to tear his mind loose from the enigma that was Gunnery Sergeant Jane Donovan.

In the barn, she'd done what had to be done. But she'd kept her distance from the boys. Then, when she'd finally joined the game, checking Pete's legs for any breaks, there had been that fleeting spark of empathy in her soft blue eyes.

Something about these kids got to her, and he had a gut feeling that, with her background, it was going to be important to find out what it was. What he couldn't do was let arrogance trip him up like it had with Nate.

Going over in his mind how he could take advantage of their sudden appearance to help Jane, he retraced his steps to the tiny cubicle of a room where he'd left the boys. An older woman emerged from the holding room next to Pete's. Her hand was bandaged. She was old enough to be his grandma.

"Are you the fella from Seattle who bought the old Anderson place?" Her tone couldn't have been more hostile.

"Yes, ma'am, I am."

Her gray eyes narrowed. "I'm Maxine Connor. Your neighbor. What are you planning to do with the place?"

So this was Gus's unmanageable Maxine.

Chase shrugged. He wasn't in the mood to talk about his

plans. Especially since he didn't have any, except to clear the place of the kids he'd unexpectedly acquired. After that, he'd go back to work making the ranch livable, maybe boarding horses and a cow or two.

"You're a city boy. Do you know how to run a working ranch?"

A picture of Jane repairing fences at his side flashed through his mind. "I'm sure I can learn."

"I'll buy it from you as is. Give you a fair price."

"I'm not interested in selling." That much he knew for certain. Maxine scowled at him. "It can get mighty cold here in the winter."

And lonely.

Chase frowned. He was plenty comfortable with his own company. "That won't be a problem."

A thump came from the open door of Pete's cubicle, followed by a stern shushing sound blending with the busy noises of the ER Department.

"Are those your children?"

Pretty sure the boys were working on a fast getaway, Chase wondered how he could end this conversation without offending the woman.

Maxine took his hesitation as assent. "Well. This is good country to raise a family in," she said gruffly before leaving him standing there, his mind whirling.

Until he could prove he wasn't a careless son-of-a-gun who'd never again put his own selfish needs before the welfare of those he'd been charged to take care of, *a family* was definitely out of the question.

Besides, in his book, making this fictional family would require a wife. He didn't have anyone lined up for the job.

Jane was sleeping peacefully. Her short hair littering the pillow like small sunbeams caused a small earthquake under his feet. Locking his jaw, he took a step to see what the boys were up to.

Jane Donovan did not have a starring role in his future. When he was done with her—he was already formulating a plan to move the woman on her way—the last thing she'd want would be to stay forever. Faster than if he lit a fire under her gorgeous behind, she'd be on the road back to the life she'd come from.

Just as he'd suspected, when he stepped into the room, Pete was already on his feet, leaning on crutches the nurse had found in a back room. "Good, you're ready to go."

A short time later, the boys were settled in the back. Glancing over at the woman riding shotgun, he pointed the Ford toward home.

Her head resting against the headrest, Jane's remarkable eyes were closed. The hard knot that had settled in his chest the night his mom told him Nate was in the hospital eased off a little. In the rearview mirror, Bobby and Pete nodded off, their heads bobbing gently at the unevenness of the road.

Jane stirred. "You're keeping me awake. I can hear you thinking clear over here."

Her voice was low, laced with a tiredness that pulled at Chase's gut. Of all the women he'd known and casually dated over the years, why did this one have to be the one who jump-started his engine like a flame lighting a firecracker?

Distraction—that's what he needed. He grasped at the first thing that came to mind. "You must have gone to parochial school."

"For twelve years. Do you ever stop working?"

Yeah. That night, Nate attempted suicide because he couldn't get hold of me.

Fatigue and the Marine's sarcasm were tinder to the fragile hold he had on his temper. He wanted her gone, so he pushed back. "I'll bet you were a wild child."

She shifted and rolled her head to look at him. "Wilder than you can imagine."

He could imagine quite a lot.

In the dark, with only the moonlight to illuminate her finely sculpted profile, those baby blues stared suspiciously at him. For a moment, all he could think about was dragging the woman across the console that divided the front seat to tuck her under his arm where she'd be safe and out of harm's way.

Respect for her rights as a patient pulled him away from the razor edge of that cliff. Suddenly, fascination's claws bit deep. "Bad girl stuff?"

Her quick snort triggered a cascade that ended up exploding in a place he would have preferred it didn't. Warning bells clanged in his head. Hot blood pumped at the provocative look she sent him. "I wasn't a good girl."

He leashed the unexpected desire pounding in his veins. The woman had come to him for help. "What did Sister Mary Margaret have to say about all this bad girl stuff?"

Her self-satisfied look pooled low in his gut. She leaned toward him with a flirty whisper, "Put your notepad away, Dr. Russell. I made sure she didn't find out."

He cleared his throat and fought to keep the seriously crazy need to touch her—even a benign touch, like pushing taunting blonde strands behind her ear—under control. "Have you seen her since you've been home?"

"No." Her arresting face became an unreadable mask as

she moved back to her side of the car, leaving him feeling unreasonably lonely. "Have you decided what to do about the boys?"

Stunned by how much he wanted that other laughing Jane back, he couldn't believe how close he was to starting something he couldn't finish.

"No."

Tightly gripping the steering wheel, he straightened his arms, pushing his shoulders into the seat. A professional relationship with Jane was vital. Otherwise, the last thing his life would be is simple.

SIX

S ome habits were just too hard to break. Despite the late hour of their return from the hospital, Jane's internal clock woke her as early as any morning she was due to report to her office at the base. That today and the days ahead were an exception to her normal routine didn't matter.

Groaning, she rolled to her back. Maybe Russell would cut them all a break. Let them sleep in. Not that she needed special favors, but the boys did. Unwelcome worry over the two runaway kids and what could happen to them intruded into the twitter of a family of birds outside her bedroom window.

Her skin heating with embarrassment, she remembered her last interaction with Russell. What was she thinking, flirting with the man? He was her therapist, not a boy toy.

One minute, she'd been working off her anxiety by wearing a rut into the pavement outside the Emergency Room. Next, she'd let her guard down and enjoyed teasing the serious man. That was until he asked if she'd seen Sister Mary Margaret since returning stateside.

How many times had she started to call the nun but hadn't?

Her guilt-laden mind skipped back to Russell and the unsettling realization that he was the first man in a long time to make her think of more than just doing her job.

Finishing her assignment so she could point her Jeep back down the road she'd come in on wasn't the only thing going on here. She didn't like it. She'd come to the ranch to get well. And to make sense of the confusion keeping her from the perfect performance of her duty. Why couldn't she keep her mind on that task and do what she did best—follow orders? Or not?

Unwilling to answer that question and favoring her hip, Jane eased out of bed, grabbed a clean T-shirt, and pulled it over her head.

What did Russell plan to do with Bobby and Pete? The obvious course of action was to turn them over to the state. There were laws about reporting runaway kids, laws she remembered too well from her days at the orphanage.

But was that the right thing to do?

Shelter and protect the lost and abandoned – that was the creed the nuns had instilled in her from the moment she'd gotten to the orphanage. They'd done it so well that it'd gotten her into trouble in Madrid.

Getting involved in Bobby and Pete's plight so soon after the incident that had landed her here in the first place was one more nail in the coffin suffocating her. Still, she couldn't shake the stubborn notion that Russell should keep the boys here. On the ranch. Where they'd be safe.

Jane shoved her legs into jeans and nicotine gum into her pocket. "Leave it be. It's none of your business," she whispered for the millionth time.

When she opened the door, the man brewing the chaos in her mind leaned on the door jam, one hand raised to knock. She jerked on the hem of the shirt she didn't quite have pulled down. His eyes locked on her bare skin, taking on a heated spark.

Her stomach clenched. "I, uh, was coming to find you."

"Good. You're up. I need you to keep an eye out for the boys." They spoke at the same time.

He needed her? Jane's mind went blank. Feeling ridiculously like a girl with her first crush, she had to call on years of rigorous training to clear the mists of lust from her mind. "Are you going to turn them over to the state?"

"I don't know yet. That would be the logical...and legal... thing to do."

She pressed her lips together. Letting her concern over Bobby and Pete take precedence was crazy, but one more penetrating glance from Dr. Chase Russell down the length of her body had logic flying out the window.

For no good reason, she wanted to be on this man's team— the other half of a two-some, worried about the welfare of two homeless boys.

"They need a bath and food. I found clothes in the attic." His voice was compellingly dangerous.

When she did not attempt to take the bundle he held out, the Doc settled in as though he could spend all day blocking her way.

Edgy and a little breathless, she pushed a lock of stray hair behind her ear. "You're thinking they're going to make a run for it."

"Wouldn't you? If you'd rather, I can get them into the bath, and you can fix breakfast."

It took scarcely a second to compare Russell's cooking with her feeble efforts. Unless there was a cafe nearby, open for breakfast and serving takeout, he was out of luck if he expected something edible from her culinary skills.

She took the clothes and towels. "You cook."

His grin was smug as he headed for the stairs. "Consider them homework."

Homework? If she wasn't as concerned as Russell about the boys making a run for it, she'd call him back and set him straight. She'd had enough *homework* in Madrid. Look how that had turned out.

She propped her back against the wall opposite Bobby and Pete's room. Popping a piece of the nicotine gum into her mouth, she waited. Patiently. Sort of.

Finally, the boy's door scraped open. Pete leaned heavily on Bobby's arm. Their shoes, the laces tied together, hung around their necks.

"Going somewhere?"

Startled, they looked up, wearing identical crap-we've-been-caught expressions. If she wasn't just as determined to keep her distance from the boys as she was to keep them here with Russell, Jane would have found it funny. But she wasn't on vacation; she had a job to do. That the assignment was her recovery made it more important than anything else she'd been ordered to do so far.

"Time for a bath."

"We don't want a bath," Bobby balked.

Jane wrinkled her nose. "You need one. When was the last time you got cleaned up?"

They stared at her in stubborn silence. Jane stared back. She knew how to play this game.

"We don't have clean clothes," Bobby informed her with enough fight. She had to give the boy points for effort.

"Russell found something for you to wear while he gets yours washed. You have twenty minutes to square yourselves away before I come in and give you a hand."

God, she sounded like the Colonel.

Glaring, Bobby grabbed the stack she held, changed directions, and awkwardly maneuvered Pete into the bathroom. Once his little brother was in, he glared at her, then shoved the door closed.

Jane smiled. So, she hadn't lost her touch. For the first time in a long time, she thought maybe Sister Mary Margaret would be proud of her.

"I'll come in and collect your clothes once you're in the tub. Don't get Pete's cast wet," she called through the door.

Her self-congratulations lasted until she heard the sharp snick of the lock. She snorted. Well, well. The teen had spunk. And nerve. That was good. He was going to need it. She'd seen plenty of kids like Bobby at the orphanage. He had the aggressiveness of someone who'd been in and out of the system for years.

Pete, on the other hand, seemed less touched by that life, but the little guy made it clear he loved and trusted his older brother. If her guess was correct, Bobby had been taking care of his younger sibling for a long time. They were family.

Jane swallowed hard, then straightened. She'd accomplished the task Russell had assigned her, preventing any attempt the boys might have made to slip away.

The last thing she wanted, and the last thing Bobby and Pete needed, was for her to hang around in the empty hallway, getting involved in their lives.

~ * ~

Chase watched Jane through the kitchen window as she made her way across the ranch yard toward the barn. She limped, but it wasn't as pronounced as when she'd first arrived.

When she'd come downstairs and informed him the boys were locked in the bathroom, her defenses were firmly locked in place. His attempt to lull her into opening up was met with stubborn silence.

After finishing the stack of pancakes and bacon he had put in front of her, she put her plate in the dishwasher, then, staring straight ahead as though reporting to her superior, informed him she'd be in the barn. All that was missing was a smart-ass salute.

It irritated him that bit of unemotional, military formality. He should be glad she was out of his way so he could concentrate on what to do with Bobby and Pete.

After what he'd seen of her trim waist and that flash of satin skin when she'd opened her bedroom door, he wanted more than just that brief view. Of course, he wouldn't pursue it, so why was it so hard to get rid of the idea?

Because Jane Donovan is a hard-headed, contradicting, conflicted, fascinating lady. That's why, he growled under his breath.

She'd been on a fishing expedition when she asked about the boys. She didn't like his answer. Her sudden interest had him taking another look at the half-formed plan he'd been mulling over of turning the boys over to Beth.

He was about to go see what was keeping them when the Marine slowed, then pivoted sharply. Suspicion pricking the back of his neck, Chase leaned forward to see what had caught her attention.

Swearing, he stepped out onto the porch.

Making for a trail that cut through the lower pasture, Bobby hovered over Pete, who clumsily used the crutches they'd gotten at the hospital. They must have slipped down the stairs while he was distracted by Jane, descending into the living room where they could escape without being seen.

He started after them. A movement from Jane stopped him. She'd put on her sunglasses, the ones that gave her that cocky, dangerous look, before sauntering toward the boys as if her hip didn't bother her at all.

Thumbs tucked in the front pockets of her jeans, she raised her chin to a rakish angle. His traitorous pulse spiked, keeping pace with her calculated steps. Bewitched, despite his best efforts not to get caught, he stepped under the shadowed canopy of the apple tree.

Well, hell. Would he turn Bobby and Pete over to a system that didn't always work as well as it should? A crazy idea taking shape, he decided to wait and see how the Marine handled the boy's bid for freedom.

~ * ~

Keep them from running. The refrain repeated itself over and over in Jane's head.

Why? Her pesky heart demanded sharply.

She knew the answer. Growing up at the orphanage, she'd often been given the newcomers to look after. The Marine Corps had reinforced the nuns' teaching with its unwritten code to serve and win battles.

A swagger she'd all but forgotten from her teenage days resurrected itself. "Where are you boys off to?"

Bobby and Pete eyed her warily, unearthing unwanted memories of how little she'd trusted anyone at their age and how little that had changed over the years.

"We...um gotta go." Bobby, his hands balling into fists, planted himself between her and his little brother.

The June sun overhead promised a hot day. The dirt beneath her boots was hard-packed. A yellow, very pregnant cat slunk out of the barn, off on a hunt through the tall grasses of the pasture.

"It's a long walk to town from here." Taking off her glasses, she squatted, resting her elbows on her knees as she swung the shades in slow circles. "You boys got traveling money?"

Bobby wasn't about to give anything away, but she could see his mind moving frantically through his options.

This is what got a person into trouble. Every time. This feeling of being responsible. Of wanting to help. Not being able to walk away. Secretly not wanting to turn out like her mother.

She should be grateful Kimberly Donovan—that was her mother's name, though she had no face to go with it—hadn't left her daughter in the garbage bin just down the block from the orphanage. She should be glad the strung-out woman had somehow found the willpower to make it to the orphanage door and ring the bell. A much younger Sister Mary Margaret had taken them both in, but it hadn't taken Kimberly long to decide she preferred the streets and drugs to her baby girl.

Jane sneered. As a teenager, knowing there was little even her mother had found to love about her, she'd flirted with a life that made Kimberly's look like a walk in the park. The day she woke up in a stranger's bed, without a single memory of how she'd gotten there, was the day she decided to change roads. It was also the day she enlisted in the Corps.

With a scowl, she firmly disconnected from the old emotions

on every level. That was water under the bridge, and she was long gone from it. "Do you know where you're going?"

Bobby's brows slammed together. His young face was an open book. Jane used his overdeveloped sense of responsibility against the boy. "How far are you going to get with your brother dragging that cast around?"

And who will take care of you? A question she couldn't ask without getting the boy's hackles up. Giving him time to think about it, she glanced down at her nails and studied them. They were cut straight across, with not a lick of polish. The cuticles were smooth and tidy.

She made her voice just as tidy, as though the boys' welfare hadn't that instant become very important to her. "You *could* stay here."

"No!"

"Russell will let you stay." She stood and locked gazes with the man who'd approached, as quiet as a sniper, behind the boys. They hadn't noticed, but Jane had been acutely aware of him from the moment he'd stepped out of the house. "Won't you?"

"They can stay." He said it with a cautious edge, but like he meant it. His willingness to play along opened up a Pandora's box she didn't want to have anything to do with.

Bobby's mouth turned down in scathing distrust. He motioned for Pete to start moving.

Jane outflanked the teenager to clamp a hand on the little tyke's shoulder, holding Pete in place. Eventually, the boys might find themselves alone and homeless in a dangerous world, but not on her watch.

Her sore heart fluttered at the understanding gleam in Russell's eyes. Her free hand slid into a fist.

His too-perceptive gaze cut to Bobby, but not before a wish that things could be different slipped free of Jane's tight restraint.

SEVEN

The next day, he bellied up to his desk to get some work done. A cup of black coffee cooled at Chase's elbow while he considered his next move. He'd thought his days of planning treatment strategies were over, yet here he was, working to individualize one for the Marine. That he'd accidentally stumbled across serious ammunition to fight her demons so early in the game was a stroke of pure luck on his part.

He cursed under his breath. When had Jane stopped being his uncle's Marine and become a woman badly in need of his help? Was it when she'd put on airs and sauntered toward the boys, her real intentions hidden beneath that sexy swagger of hers? No.

Maybe it was the moment she'd squatted down at their level and talked to them like equals, as if being there, at that moment, was all that mattered.

He shook his head at the seductive image. Not that either.

"Russell, you are one unlucky son," he muttered, rising to

stand at the window.

It was when he'd come up behind the boys. Though he could tell she knew he was there, her attention remained firmly fixed on Bobby and Pete, her questions not pushing, just curious as she coaxed them into staying. All the while, her thoughts had been directed inward. The isolation she found there littered her gorgeous eyes, betraying a fearful inner landscape.

He was snared. Well and truly. He would do everything he could to help her. Not because his uncle willed it, but because he'd unfortunately discovered there was more to Jane Donovan than the stoic Marine who'd been sent for him to heal.

Simply put, she intrigued him. There was an intriguing woman hidden beneath all the layers of protection she'd wrapped herself in, and much to his dismay, he wanted to be the one to bring her out of hiding.

Gus poked his head into the office. "Bad news, Boss. I just got off the phone with Jim Bartlett. He just sold the last of his horses to another buyer."

After his run-in at the hospital with his neighbor, Chase had been vaguely toying with, someday, turning the place into some kind of working ranch, but mulling over the treatment plan he was developing for Jane, a crazier idea came to mind. "Do you know anyone else who has horses to sell? Sweet-natured, gentle animals?"

"Maxine Connor has the sweetest animals in the county. She breaks them in real gentle like."

Maxine Connor. Of course. Sighing, he gave in to the inevitable. "Let's go see her, then."

"What about the youngsters?"

"Jane can keep an eye on them. Are they still in the barn?"

Gus raised bushy brows. "Yup. They finished cleaning up

the tack room. When I left, they were sweeping out stalls."

Grinning, he went to give the Marine the good news that she would be playing babysitter. When he stepped into the cool interior of the large building, the murmur of voices drew him past the stalls to the back of the cavernous building.

"You boys do good work. How old are you?" Jane's quiet, calming tone would coax a grown man out of his last beer. Chase stopped in the shadow of a sturdy support beam to listen.

"Six." Pete scrubbed his greasy hands on his pant legs. Jane handed the little guy a rag.

Bobby was slower to come up to scratch. "Thirteen." his voice cracked on the last syllable, making him flush.

Chase was impressed with how little effort it took Jane to get useful information from the runaways. He straightened. The woman was more dangerous than the incendiary device that nearly took her out in Madrid.

"You boys in need of a job? I'm sure Russell could use some extra hands around here." Amused blue eyes pinned him, her smile full of mocking humor. His heart did a sudden backflip.

He rubbed the ache at the back of his neck. Pete's frail thinness, Bobby's wary determination to protect his little brother no matter what, and the Marine's cockiness made it nearly impossible to ignore her challenge to make room for the boys on the ranch.

How long could he reasonably expect to keep the brothers safely off the streets? He was going to find out. He'd play her game for the time being. But by his own rules.

Knowing what was there, he looked past Jane. "Did you find the motorcycle?"

Jane shrugged as though it were no big thing, but there was a glow of excitement in her eyes that hadn't been there when she first arrived on the ranch. "A Harley. Sweet machine. Looks like it's been abandoned."

"It was here when I bought the place. Must have been left by the previous owners."

She looked longingly at the big bike. "I'd love to buy this baby from you."

The sudden wish that she'd look at him with the same longing was completely irrational. But mixed with the sweet scent of vanilla she wore, the sharp smell of used motor oil and hay, the volatile combination had his blood pumping big time.

Get a grip, buddy. "I'm sure we can come to some kind of arrangement." Dragging his attention away from the sexy lady, Chase addressed the boys. "I'll pay good wages if you're willing to work hard."

"You'd pay us?" The cautious hope sprouting on Bobby's face was one more link in the chain binding Chase to a situation he would have bet, just that morning, he would have had no intention of shouldering.

He shouldn't do it. There would be ramifications down the road he couldn't immediately foresee. But it was too late to change his mind. Deep in his gut, he knew Jane needed these kids as much as they needed a safe place to land.

"I expect a good day's work."

Bobby hesitated, but not for long. "Okay, Mister, you've got a deal."

Jane's look of approval lured him in. About to dive headfirst into those compelling blues of hers, he pulled himself back just in time. "I have to go see about some horses. I want you to watch the boys."

The sassy smirk left her face. "That's not part of our deal."

"It is now. You know the homework I mentioned earlier? We'll discuss what it entails when I get back."

Sidestepping the picture of an unlikely family that mushroomed in his head, with ground-eating strides, Chase walked as quickly as possible away from the scowling lady Marine, who was making a minefield of the simple, quiet life he'd left Seattle and a thriving practice to find.

~ * ~

"Bobby and Pete were asleep before their heads hit the pillow. I appreciate you watching them for me today."

He'd crept up on her. Jane opened her eyes at the husky voice that scraped an unwanted tremor of need up her spine. He leaned against the porch railing, his feet crossed at the ankles, arms folded over his chest. The snaps of his shirt were open, revealing a sprinkle of dark hair.

She gave the porch swing a firm push. She was not going to fall into the trap of being charmed by her therapist. She was on the ranch to get whole and healthy so she could return to her duties, prepared to handle any situation the Corps threw at her.

In the meantime, to stay on her toes, she had no qualms about lobbing a few shells into the Doc's camp. "You didn't give me much choice."

He met her accusation with a level gaze. "No, I suppose I didn't."

Thunder clapped overhead, followed quickly by fat drops of rain plopping on the roof of the porch. The sound wrapped them in a cozy intimacy that had a faint flush warming her cheeks.

"Did you get the horses?"

"The lady's thinking it over."

Lady? Out of nowhere, jealousy pricked Jane, which made no sense. Chase Russell didn't belong to her in that way and never would. Quickly dismissing the unreasonable resentment, she raised an inquiring eyebrow.

"My next door neighbor, Maxine Connor, has a few horses to sell. She's just not all that keen on selling them to a city boy." For the first time since she had met him, Russell smiled. A genuine smile that made it to his gorgeous eyes, then he reached out to her. "Her words. Not mine."

Her stomach plummeted. She gave the rocker another push, determined not to notice how truly hot the man was with his jeans riding low and his feet bare.

"You could get them from someone else."

"I could, but Gus says Maxine has the sweetest horses in the area." He paused, then, without explaining why that was important, changed the subject entirely. "You were good with the boys this morning."

She shrugged. "I've had a little experience."

"At the orphanage?"

Jane stared at him. Russell was just doing what he'd agreed to do. His job.

"Sister Mary Margaret liked the older kids to help out."

On a sudden, crazy impulse, she left the swing and joined him at the railing. Her thigh brushed his. A spark of acute awareness snapped along sensitized nerves like a loose high-voltage wire. She sucked in a breath as his outdoorsy, woodsy scent pushed her into wanting more.

Don't be stupid. She shoved her hands into her front pockets.

"Were you ever able to find out anything about your mom or her family?" Russell's smoky tone was easy, more like one friend talking to another than a counselor engaged in talk therapy with his client, which was what this little impromptu conversation had turned into.

Everything about Chase Russell was unexpected. His clean, good looks. The way he reluctantly took lost souls under his protective wing. How he was looking at her now, as though he was interested in Jane the person, not just Jane the wounded Marine he had to fix.

Didn't the Doc know he was supposed to set a time and place for these little chats, not pounce on her whenever the whim struck?

"There's nothing to know. When it was more important for my mother to get her next fix than it was to be a mom, she left. And she didn't leave behind any *dear daughter* letters to explain why she left me with strangers." She pushed away from the railing, the man, and the memories.

He stopped her with a restraining hand, fanning the heat curling in her belly. One finger stroked her jaw, leaving a trail of fiery maelstrom in its wake. "I'm sorry."

Tired of fighting her attraction, she gave him a crooked smile. "You don't have to be. That was a long time ago, and the Corps is my family now."

His hands dropped as his brows came together. "That's good." He didn't look convinced.

Perhaps it'd been a mistake to think she could go toe-to-toe with Russell and not get burned. In her defense, she was fighting a war on three fronts. "What's this homework you mentioned?"

"Like I said, you did a good job watching over the boys today. Your *homework,* should you decide to take it—" Humor eased the frown from his handsome face. "—is to find out their real names and where they came from."

From somewhere deep inside, Jane came a sudden wish that the man wasn't her therapist. It would be a novelty to be the girl next door with no worries. The one who was dating the hunky neighbor guy.

She'd never had the chance to be that fresh, innocent girl, whose dream was a picket fence and a family of her very own that included a husband she could count on and love to distraction. And while she was dreaming big, why not add four happy children, a cat, and two dogs to the picture?

But she wasn't that girl.

Gunny, step away from the good doctor.

Intending to put some distance between her and the unlikely image he seemed to have of her as the boys' guardian angel and the illusion that they could all make one big happy family, she edged away from Russell.

She'd meant it sincerely when she'd promised herself she would jump through any hoop he asked her to, but that hadn't included taking on two runaway kids who needed more help than she was capable of giving. Or becoming responsible for getting strategic intel from them.

What reason could she give for not taking on the assignment Russell was so eager to give? "I don't think that's a good idea." She was interrupted by the sound of a vehicle coming down the drive.

In the dark, headlights bobbed. A road-weary Dodge truck parked next to her Jeep. Then, Sergeant Scott Boone unfolded his tall, lanky length from the rig.

Russell pushed away from the porch rail. "Do you know him?"

"Yes." She moved to the bottom step and waited.

"Gunny," Boone greeted her, as serious as a lead pipe in the hands of a skilled fighter. His gaze flicked to Russell for a brief second, then zeroed in on her.

"What are you doing here, Sergeant?"

"You're off the grid. The guys got worried. We decided someone had to come find you. I drew the short straw."

Jane folded her arms across her chest. *The guys* were her Friday night poker buddies in Madrid. Embarrassment flooded her. She'd shut them out. Disconnected entirely.

"How did you find me?"

"Your CO."

Jane's self-imposed isolation unraveled a bit at the thought of Boone going out of his way to hunt her down.

Russell shifted beside her, and she couldn't help but compare the two men. The Doc won, hands down.

They were similar in many ways, height, good looks, but Boone's military bearing had nothing on Russell's honed physique. And, over late-night beers, she'd discovered long ago, the Sergeant wasn't the settling-down type. Hell, none of them were.

Russell, on the other hand, had responsible written all over his fine form. That was her problem. It was like putting nectar under the beak of a migrating hummingbird.

"Sergeant Scott Boone, this is Dr. Chase Russell. He—" She wasn't ready to go into the details of her situation with Russell. "—owns this ranch."

The men eyed each other warily.

Jane stepped between them. "How long can you stay?"

"A few hours. I have to report in by eighteen-hundred tomorrow."

A stab of jealousy attacked her. While she was stuck here,

Boone was heading to a new assignment. "How about some coffee?"

"That would be great."

In the kitchen, Russell waved her off. "I'll get the coffee. You go visit."

She flashed him a smile, then settled at the table across from the Sergeant. Boone lounged comfortably in the chair, his elbow hitched over the back rail. He studied her with a deceptively casual look. "What are you doing here?"

Her gaze darted to Russell. He cocked his head sideways, waiting to see what she was going to tell her buddy.

The long, awkward silence stretched out. What was she supposed to say? *I'm a nut case, so I've been marooned here until I get better?*

Boone caught on without words and quickly picked up the slack. The sympathy in his too-knowing eyes made Jane want to strike out. Good thing she was past that kind of behavior, she sneered.

"So, Friday night poker isn't the same without you. Bear's been on a roll. Can't beat the dude."

Russell put steaming cups in front of them, then retreated to the other side of the island that separated the kitchen from the dining area. He leaned against the counter, his cup in hand. Jane followed his movements before jerking her attention back to Boone.

"How?" She swallowed at the amusement in her buddy's eyes. She wanted to deny any perceived attraction to Russell, but she knew Boone, the player, wouldn't believe it. She cleared her throat. "How are Bear and Lacey doing? Any more incidents after?"

Boone shook his head. "No. It's been quiet since you left.

Took a while to get things cleaned up, but we've kept security tight, and the dust has settled."

Jane divorced herself from her role in the bombing; let the warm memories of being with her comrades roll over her. The conversation shifted to safer ground.

Three hours passed too quickly. Through it all, Russell hung out in the background. She was oddly comforted by his presence.

Before she knew it, Boone was climbing back into his rig. He hesitated before strapping himself in. "Stop blaming yourself for what happened, Gunny. And don't stay out here in the middle of nowhere too long. Lacey said to tell you she hasn't had a decent game since you left. She wants to plan a weekend in Vegas as soon as she and Bear get stateside."

"I'll see what I can do."

He gave her his charmer's smile, the one he used on all potential girlfriends, but it did nothing more for Jane than make her think of the man in the house whose grin was a killer.

Pulling the door closed, he tossed her a jaunty two-fingered salute. "Stay in touch."

"Will do." For the first time, she meant it.

During Boone's short stay, he'd reminded her she wasn't as lost as she thought. She had good friends who weren't blaming her for what happened.

As the silence of the night closed around her, the constant anxiety she'd been carrying for so long eased just a little.

~ * ~

Over the next couple of days, Chase made sure he had no opportunity to be alone with the enticing Marine. It was an easy task since it seemed she didn't want to be alone with him either.

He couldn't explain it. He'd wanted to kiss her. Despite his better judgment. And, to heck with the rules. If it hadn't been for the arrival of her fellow Marine, he just might have given in to the overwhelming desire to drag her close, take in her sweet scent, and explore the soft skin right where her elegant neck met her shoulder.

Lucky for them both, they'd been interrupted. He'd watched her with Sergeant Boone and gotten a glimpse of what her life in the Marine Corps must have been like. She might have cut off all contact with those she'd served with in Spain, but contrary to what she thought, the woman wasn't friendless. Scott, Lacey, and the one called Bear all cared about her and were anxious to have her back.

She'd visibly relaxed in Scott's company in a way he'd never gotten her to do. Jealousy twisted into something dark in Chase's gut until he remembered there had been no physical contact between Jane and the other Marine. Not even when it was time for Boone to leave.

Determined to get back to work, he threw on some workout clothes, then searched for the woman until he found her at the punching bag. No surprise there. He pulled on gloves and joined her.

Hands dropping to her sides, she took a few dancing steps, her limp barely noticeable. Her heaving chest mocked his resolve to hang onto a measure of reasonable professional conduct. Sweat glistened on her tanned skin. Corn-silk hair stuck up in sexy matted spikes. Hastily, he promised himself he would not give in to the attraction battering him like boiling rapids during a white water rafting trip on the nearby Deschutes River.

"I want to try something new."

"Okay." She eyed him suspiciously. He couldn't blame her.

"It's called recreational therapy. A camping trip. You. Me. The boys."

As Jane considered his plan, she joined him in a punishing attack on the punching bag. Amidst the thud of their gloves against the swaying bag, they settled into a steady rhythm that had him admiring her grace under fire and her complete devotion to the task at hand.

"I know what you're up to." The pull of her brows together didn't disguise the fragile vulnerability she was usually extremely good at hiding.

That peek beyond her staunch defenses had him wishing he could hold her and offer comfort without worrying about what kind of therapist that would make him. Which led to wondering what it would be like to have her looking at him with a lusty ambush on her mind.

"What am I up to?"

"You think by forcing me to spend time with the boys, hoping it'll initiate a breakthrough. You're hoping it will help me understand what I did wrong in Madrid." She said that without a lick of emotion, as if she were an outside observer looking in, without the slightest internal attachment to the riotous feelings that had to be swirling in her chest.

"According to the report I read, you didn't do anything wrong in Madrid."

Putting her whole weight behind the next jab, she snorted, making him almost miss his next punch. "How do you know?"

"Know what?"

"That I didn't lie for the report. That I didn't make a huge mistake that cost a kid his life."

He raised his brows. "Did you lie?"

She paused for a moment before giving the bag another bone-shattering hit. "No."

Having one chance to get this right, Chase leaned around the bag so he could capture her angry gaze. "You're headstrong, arrogant, and stubborn."

Her chin hitched up. "Gee, thanks."

Behind the polite mask she wore as though hardly interested, he could see the vortex of unchained emotions churning in her beautiful eyes.

"You're also compassionate, courageous, and dedicated. You love the Corps. You'd never do anything to jeopardize your standing there."

"What if I didn't know what I was doing?" The question was a whisper. She wanted to believe him. He could see it in the desperate, still way she held herself.

His vow to stay professional slipped a notch.

"You knew what you were doing. You were leading with your heart, giving aid to a homeless kid."

She began to pull off her gloves. "Which was my first mistake and brings us right back to where we started. It was my fault Linus got killed."

"No, it doesn't. Sometimes bad things just happen."

Pressing her lips together, she dropped the gloves to the ground and lobbed a jerky nod in his direction. With her back ramrod straight, she stalked toward the barn.

Okay then, clearly this session is over.

Chase gave the bag a hard jab that reverberated up his arm.

Patience Russell. Rome wasn't built in a day.

EIGHT

J ane twisted the last bolt tight. After her session with
Russell that morning, she'd come to the barn and
deliberately put it all out of her mind.

A large part of her wanted to understand what had gone
wrong in Madrid. Another, just as demanding part, was plain
tired of herself and exhausted from rumbling over the same
old ground.

Just once, she'd like to be a normal person who wasn't falling
apart. Your average twenty-something, taking a well-deserved
vacation. For the first time in her life, she *wanted* to be one of
those silly women who had nothing better to do than pursue
a ridiculous, scintillating crush on her therapist.

Only she'd never been normal. Thinking she could start now
was a hysterically bad joke.

Russell believed she had all this courage and dedication—
two things she'd be lucky to have when she went back on duty.
She wished she could prove his belief in her was warranted.

But how?

The only way she knew was to do everything he asked of her, no matter how childish and irrelevant it seemed. She had nothing to lose and everything to gain by playing this campaign his way.

But what if all her hard work didn't make a lick of difference? What if, after putting her trust in him, he couldn't fix her, and she had to return to base with her tail tucked between her legs, her re-enlistment denied despite all her efforts?

Jane swept the disabling doubt from her mind. She refused to march down that road.

"Don't touch anything, guys. I'll be right back. I have some spare oil in my rig." She wiped the grime off her hands, using a rag she'd found in the tack room, then tossed it to Pete, who squatted in the straw by the rear wheel of the motorcycle. Bobby, hands poked in his pants' pockets, leaned against a nearby wall.

Jane kept the oil on hand for the Indian motorcycle she'd left back at the base. She'd acquired it secondhand and over many months, lovingly rebuilt the engine.

She missed being able to ride; she hadn't been able to since her injury. That was about to change. Stepping out of the barn into bright sunlight, by instinct alone, she just missed running straight into the man taking over her life.

"Lunch is ready. How's it going out here?" The gruff concern in his voice scuttled her thin control.

"We're about to crank her over. Just getting oil from my Jeep." She clamped her tongue between her teeth to stop babbling. He did that to her. Made her lose track of why she was here.

When she returned with the oil, he followed her, a little too closely for comfort, into the barn. "Show me."

Her steps slowed. Bobby was crouched beside his brother. Both had their backs to her.

Someday, Bobby, whoever he was, would grow into a handsome man. His love and protectiveness for his little brother would draw the girls like bees to honey. Jane wondered if things would have turned out different for her if she'd had a big brother to worry over her.

Pete scrubbed his hands on the rag she'd tossed him earlier.

Bobby watched indulgently, then shook his head. "You're such a girl, Abby."

Pete shot a look at Bobby. "You said we're not supposed to say–"

Jane pulled Chase quickly into the nearest stall. When Bobby glanced over his shoulder, he didn't see them. "That's right, but there's no one around."

Stunned by the secret the kids had hidden so well, she glanced at Russell, got caught up in the self-mockery shifting across his face, and started to fall.

"This is an unexpected development," she managed to whisper around the firecrackers going off in her chest, meaning the way the counselor was taking over her senses, not that one little boy had turned out to be a girl.

Strong hands found her waist, massaging surprisingly greedy flesh.

Stand down, Gunny. Instead, inside her belly, something very feminine stood at attention, taking notice.

"It sure is." Russell's voice was deep, jagged like the Rocky Mountains she'd driven through to get to the ranch.

She groaned, not knowing which sucked more. Finding out one of the boys was a girl and she hadn't noticed? Or, discovering that no matter how much she tried not to be, she could no longer deny she was taking more than a passing, flirty interest in her therapist.

God, the man should wear a sign. *Danger, Jane, danger.*

If she had the courage Russell claimed she did, she'd tell him right then and there what he did to her equilibrium, and what, if given half a chance, she wanted to do about it. But she lost the opportunity when he released her and moved them out of the stall.

It was crazy thinking, anyway. All she had to do was hold it together long enough for him to clear her to go home. Once she got back to base, she'd dive back into her life, maybe go on a date or two, and forget all about the handsome, sexy Doc resurrecting ideas she'd given up a long time ago.

Taking a fortifying breath, she held up the container she'd retrieved from her Jeep. "Okay, I'll add the oil, then we can start this puppy up."

Bobby stood and greeted her pronouncement with a hesitant smile. Her heart jerked. If she were at the base right now, on a Tuesday morning, she'd be doing paperwork at her desk or meeting with staff. Maybe exercising the kink out of her hip at the gym. She wouldn't, all of a sudden, be wondering what it would be like to be part of a family that included two brave kids and one seductive man.

Uncapping the oil container, she poured some of the thick, black fluid into the corresponding opening. Sorting out her priorities would be smart, but she couldn't get past the discovery that Pete was a girl. Little more than a baby, who had only her teenage brother to protect her from a world that could turn against her in a heartbeat.

Where the hell were her parents?

Did she have a mother who was worried sick about where

her daughter was?

Linus's face crowded into the mix. The orphaned street urchin had reminded her too much of herself, and she hadn't been able to turn her back on him. Now, here were these two kids, just as alone in the world, except for her and Russell.

Jane swore under her breath.

Pete, or rather Abby, jumped up with an excited hop. "Can I go for a ride?"

She told herself this wasn't Madrid. She hadn't befriended a motherless kid who would later strike at the only family she had. And, she wasn't at the orphanage anymore, in charge of kids who, as soon as she got used to having them around, found families of their own in adoption or permanent foster care.

It didn't help. A loathsome, familiar slide into panic crept in on her. She sucked in a breath to catch it before it caught hold, but the edges of her vision began to turn dark.

The Colonel was right. She *had* lost her edge.

"Please, can I go first? Can I?"

The girl's sweet voice pierced the fog engulfing Jane. She locked her jaw in a futile attempt to slow her tumble. She had to get out. Fast. Before she made a fool of herself by losing it in front of these strangers she'd somehow come to care about.

"Please?"

"Not this time. I have to take the bike for a test drive before you go for a ride."

Abby's shoulders slumped in disappointment.

Hands shaking, Jane jammed one of the helmets she'd cleaned up on her head. The other she tossed blindly to the ground.

Breathing became impossible in the confines of the barn.

Pushing the heavy bike out into the open, she quickly climbed aboard. Gripping the handlebars until her knuckles ached, she focused on one thing and one thing only. Getting away before the panic won.

Russell, carrying the helmet she'd thrown down, slipped onto the Harley behind her.

"What are you doing?"

"Going with you." He strapped on the helmet.

"The kids—"

"Will be fine with Gus."

On the edge of her numbed vision, she saw the old man leaning against the corral, one foot perched on the lower rail.

"Suit yourself." She gunned the gas; had the satisfaction of feeling the front tire come off the ground.

Dirt spewed behind them in a cloud of dust. Instead of sliding off and landing on his hot butt, Russell pressed into her back, holding on, fingers digging into her hips.

The warmth from his body only flamed the panic closing in.

He pointed. Without care for life or limb, she took the rutted forestry road he indicated.

Ruthless speed and precision reflexes finally slowed her tumble. Catching her breath, she wrestled with the dread filling her mind.

The road took them into juniper-covered hills. The man behind her swayed into the corners with her. The snug fit of his body at her back seemed shockingly natural, as if he'd been made just for her. When his hands splayed across her stomach, it nearly cost her the next curve.

She shot the bike into a small clearing, breaking hard, barely noticing the lake that sparkled just beyond in the sunlight. Flipping the kickstand down, she shut off the engine, practically tumbling sideways off the heavy machine.

Pulling off her helmet, she threw it at the ground. A well-honed instinct for survival had her spinning around to face her unwanted passenger as she plunked tight fists on her hips to keep them out of trouble.

He slowly climbed off the bike, the look in his eyes predatory. He wanted answers. Answers Jane wasn't sure she had.

After landing his helmet next to hers, arms hanging loose, he confronted her, his booted feet planted wide. "What happened back there?"

"Nothing." She went hot with embarrassment. Smoke screen. She needed a smoke screen. "So, Pete's a girl."

"So it would seem."

He waited. She scrambled for another diversion, then decided she had to throw him a bone. "I know you'll find this hard to believe, but when I was Bobby and…Abby's age, I wasn't all that popular."

"No?"

"In school, I was kind of a fringe kid."

"Had a hard time fitting in?"

She sucked in a breath to ease the tight band squeezing her chest. "Maybe they had a hard time fitting in with me?"

Amusement smoothed out the concerned lines bracketing Russell's mouth. "So, were you a big track star or a chess geek?"

She smirked, finally able to turn back some of the edges of the panic that had made her run from the barn, the kids, and the vision of a life she wouldn't know what to do with. "Detention was the sport I excelled in."

He laughed. Her stomach took a killer tumble when he narrowed the distance between them.

"Tell me what happened back there," he ordered softly.

Did she dare?

"Please." The quiet request rumbled seductively from his chest.

Jane made herself meet his compassionate look head-on. She didn't want his sympathy, but her defenses were getting pretty battered in the attempt to keep her distance. "I had a panic attack."

His penetrating gaze saw more than she wanted him to. "You haven't told anyone about them, have you?"

"No. Can you just see it? A Marine who has panic attacks going into a hot situation? They'd boot me out faster than it would take them to write discharge orders. I don't want a medical discharge. I want to go back to work."

"So you've been trying to handle this all on your own. How long have you been having these episodes?"

Whirling away from him, she blindly made it to the lake's edge, where the water gently lapped at the shore. She was oblivious to its sunlit, glass-like surface. A gentle breeze cooled her flushed skin.

"Since I got out of the hospital." She wished more than anything that the solitude of the trees surrounding the lake could erase all her troubles.

"They didn't start in Madrid?"

"No."

Russell came up behind her, so close, the musk of his soap mixed with the earthy smells of the lake. "I know some techniques that will help you get control of the attacks."

"What techniques? More play therapy?" She wanted to believe him. Spinning to face him, she tried to smile, falling desperately short of the mark.

"How to calm your mind. Uncovering what thinking

patterns cause the attacks. Finding effective ways to intercept them."

God, the woman was a fighter.

Chase watched her struggle, irrationally overcome by a sharp need to drag her close. He wanted to kiss the living daylights out of her until all the painful memories went away, but he was pretty certain she wouldn't approve of the out-of-line contact as appropriate adjunct therapy. Of course, *he* didn't either.

His uncle had sent Jane to get control of her post-traumatic stress disorder. All Chase could think about was this haunted woman who hid so much anguish beneath an impassive surface, tying him up with an overwhelming desire that demanded he help her any way he could.

It was a feeling he'd never experienced before. One he couldn't shake as it morphed into something deeper, more impossible to ignore.

A pair of birds twittered in the branches over his head. Unable to keep his hands to himself, he tucked a wisp of hair behind Jane's ear, all but forgetting that letting his emotions take over was the very last thing he should do.

"I'm going to kiss you."

"That's not a good idea."

"I know."

She reached for him. "You're my therapist."

"Which only makes this a very big mistake," he growled, brushing his lips across her parted mouth.

On what sounded like a ravenous sigh, she looped her arms around his neck and tangled her fingers in his hair. He dragged her against his chest. Trapped in her vanilla scent, he explored the pearls of her spine, dug into yielding shoulders. He persuaded her to come closer still, marveling at how perfectly she fit into his arms.

He knew what he was doing. Still had control. Just a minute longer, he bargained with the rational side of his brain while throwing aside innate caution and vaulted ethics.

Just in time, he stepped back from the precipice, laid his forehead against hers. A shaky laugh escaped his chest. "We should stop."

"You're right," she whispered before taking charge, capturing him in a meeting of lips that rocked him to his toes. A powerful drive to have her right there beside the pristine lake, with the hard ground for a bed and only the sky for covering was his undoing.

Logic and good intentions fled. He gave in to her bold, fascinating mouth; took advantage of the pulse at her temple and the sensitive skin just south of her delicate ear.

Through the fabric of her top, he cupped her firm breast, flicked his thumb across the peak begging for his attention. A need he couldn't analyze, urgent and more than just a desire for physical release, struck. It left him hard and wanting more than he should consider taking.

"I want to do more than kiss you, Angel."

Stormy blue eyes focused on him. The sun overhead sparkled off the strands of her pale hair.

"Angel?" Her voice was a distracted rasp, rough with unspent passion. A laugh broke free from her parted lips, turning his already beleaguered control to mush. "I'm no angel."

"Are you sure? You have a halo."

The timing was crappy, but suddenly it occurred to Chase he'd been missing something vital in his life. Even when he was at the top of his game in Seattle, there had been an empty place none of his former success had filled.

He dropped his hands. Sex with a beautiful, exciting woman was one thing. Getting emotionally tied up with a dyed-in-the-wool Marine who was his patient, and who would return to her unit without once looking over her shoulder, was the worst thing he could do.

"I'm sure."

This time, Jane was the one who backed off.

~ * ~

Back at the ranch house, Chase wondered who was more wounded. The two kids who'd landed on his doorstep because of whatever situation had set them on the run? The Marine who carried an internal wound deeper than the one that left her with a cranky hip? Or the ex-therapist who'd once thought he had all the answers but had nothing except an inconvenient case of the hots for a courageous lady who wouldn't hang around once he'd given her the tools to take her life back?

If he were a betting man, he'd lay down money it was him. Of course, that mind-numbing kiss had been a mistake. A setback.

This was the point where he was supposed to remind himself that Jane belonged to the United States government. And he would, as soon as he erased certain pictures from his over-fertile imagination. The first of Jane in his bed. The second, the four of them—he, Jane, and the two kids—forming an unlikely alliance, a family forged from mutual need.

The Corps didn't care that the Gunny was a fascinating, arousing woman. Now that he understood the depth of what she was dealing with, he could keep his promise to his uncle and move her along. At least that's what he told himself.

The phone at his elbow rang. He snatched it up. "Hello?"

"How's it going?"

Speak of the devil. Chase shifted the phone to his other ear, stabilizing the device with his shoulder. "Uncle Matt—"

"Is she cooperating?"

A noise at his office door brought his head up. Jane stood there, and from the stiffness of her shoulders, she had overheard the booming question.

Cooperating? He locked stares with her and immediately flashed to that moment by the lake. She must have gone to the same place because a hint of pink flooded her stunning face.

Since it wouldn't be smart to alert his uncle to his momentary dive into the forbidden, he simply said, "You could say that. She's right here. Why don't you get a progress report from her?"

Rising from his desk, he backed Jane into the hall. The kids were lined up behind her, Abby hanging onto the Marine's belt loop like it was a lifeline.

He handed the phone to Jane, his fingers scraping briefly along her palm, causing a renewal of the craving that had gotten him into trouble at the lake.

Freeing Abby from her belt and keeping the child's small, trusting hand firmly in his own, he headed down the hall. "Come on, guys. We'll fix lunch while Miss Jane takes this call."

It would be safer all around if he gave them both some space while he got a handle on his randy hormones. The last time he'd let his Johnson do his thinking for him, he'd been a teenager. Taking a tumultuous trip down memory lane wasn't an option for a grown man who was supposed to be in control of his life.

NINE

Jane couldn't take her eyes off Russell as he led the kids toward the kitchen. Okay, so she liked his kisses. Even more, she liked his clever hands on her body. But that was all.

As tempting as the notion was, and despite her fingers threading of their own accord into the soft hair at the nape of his neck, a session of therapeutic sex with her therapist wasn't part of the mission.

"Gunny, how are you doing?"

The impatience in the Colonel's voice demanded Jane's full attention. "Better."

To her surprise, it was true. Even with her recent panic attack and the attempt to will it away by losing herself in Russell's sexy embrace.

"Good. I have an assignment, I think you'll be interested in."

"I…um…need more time here." Not because of Chase Russell, she promised the voice snorting in her head.

"You still have time. I want you in tip-top shape when you come back."

Her mind wrapping around the discovery that she wasn't chafing at the bit to rush home, Jane carried the phone into the kitchen. When she got there, lunch was forgotten, since Russell was heading out the back door, the kids close on his heels.

"Yes, Sir."

She followed them out, stopping at the edge of the porch, enjoying the view of the Doc's long strides eating up the distance to a heavy-duty truck parked by the corral. Gus was already there, talking to a lady.

"Take care of yourself, Gunny. And make sure my nephew doesn't turn into a hermit out there."

Russell motioned for Bobby and Abby to stay back.

"I don't think there's much chance of that, Sir."

"Good. Keep me apprised of your progress." The line to her old life disconnected.

She idly wondered what the Colonel was up to, but didn't have time to figure it out. She was more curious about what was going on between the woman and Russell as they squared off.

After returning the phone to the kitchen, she joined the kids. "What's happening?"

Abby grabbed her hand. "That's Mr. Russell's neighbor."

The woman was dressed in well-worn jeans and a practical western shirt, sleeves rolled up to her elbows, and boots worn and dusty. A straw hat covered most of her short hair.

It didn't look like it was the state of the union they were discussing.

The gal's chin hitched to a stubborn angle. The anger in her voice carried. "I'm not here to sell you horses. I wanted to try one more time to persuade you to sell me your ranch."

So, this was Russell's *lady*. The one he was in negotiations with to sell him horses.

"Now, Maxine—" Gus placed a placating hand on the woman's shoulder.

The bits of hair poking out from beneath her hat were salt and pepper gray. The crow's feet at the corners of her shrewd eyes cut deep, her skin tan and weathered like she'd spent a lot of time out in the elements. Maxine Connor was older than the contained energy her wiry frame hinted at. She visibly melted at Gus' touch.

A sprig of envy shot through Jane. Russell's neighbor was in love. With Gus. At an age when it seemed as though that elusive emotion should have stopped screwing around with the old girl's heart.

"Gus, honey, you know this is ranch country, not a play-ground for bored city folk."

"Ms. Connor, I'm not selling." Russell ground out, his determination to stay put bringing up a longing Jane shouldn't be having.

"You'll change your mind," Maxine said, then spun around to head for her vehicle.

His thick, white brows slammed together. Gus followed after her. "Maxine, now wait a darn minute."

The older woman climbed into her truck, waved jauntily at Gus, then drove off. Her tires kicked up gravel on the way out.

"That went well," Russell muttered, placing a hand on Bobby's shoulder when he joined him.

For the first time in her career, Jane found herself disagree-ing with a superior officer. Hermit or not, Russell belonged on this ranch. With these kids. Bobby and Abby looking up at him like he was their hero suited him.

Deep down in her heart sprang a secret wish that she belonged here, too. That somehow she'd managed to find her hero.

She went still. Okay, that was way off base. Maybe she wasn't doing as well as she thought.

~ * ~

The next morning, Chase crossed his fingers that his long-time friend Beth Greeley would see things his way. How many times in the course of their Human Psychology studies in college had they debated the merits of the current social services structure, agreeing that more community involvement could only make the system better?

After graduation, with her optimism and drive to make lasting changes, Beth went to work in the Department of Human Services, working her way to the top rung. Now, his study buddy headed up the Crook County Child Welfare Department. She was the only one who could help Bobby and Abby.

After spending a restless night between dreams of taking up where he and Jane had left off at the lake and worrying about what to do with Bobby and Abby, he woke up early to see if he could talk Beth into letting him keep the kids at the ranch. At least until a better solution presented itself.

If in the process it helped the Marine with her recovery, chalk one up for him. He frowned. She was a lot of work. Maybe more than a lot.

So were Bobby and Abby. But the truth was, some time since the children's arrival, he'd discovered he didn't want to turn them over to a system that might not have their best interests at heart.

And to be honest, in the darkness of a sleepless night, he'd realized he had answers to find—no surprise. He had an unsettling feeling that these kids and one feisty Marine could help him.

He dialed the number Beth had given him when she found out he'd bought a place in her county. An assistant took his name and put him through to her office.

"Chase. What a delight. I hope you're calling to make a lunch date."

"Lunch would be great, but that's not why I called. I need a favor."

"Does it have anything to do with the woman you've got staying at your place?"

"How do you know about her?"

"News travels fast in a small town."

Chase gulped his lukewarm coffee. "Gunnery Sergeant Jane Donovan. She's here on leave."

"A girlfriend you haven't told me about?"

"A job for my Uncle."

"Really." The one word was ripe with speculation.

Chase refused to discuss the Marine. It was bad enough he couldn't keep her out of his dreams without fighting daytime fantasies as well.

"She's not why I called."

"Too bad. But, if you ever want dating advice—" It was an old offer that went way back. Married now with a kid of her own, Beth thought he should join the club.

"I've got two runaway kids staying here."

Without breaking stride, she went from a teasing friend to a focused professional. "Where did they come from?"

"I'm still trying to find out. I've threatened to chain them in the dungeon, but so far, they won't tell."

Beth laughed. "What are their names?"

"They're going by Bobby and Pete Jones. We found out yesterday the younger one is a girl, Abby."

"We?"

Chase ignored her curious probing. "They're brother and sister."

"When can you bring them in?"

"That's the thing. I want to keep them here. Just until we figure out who they are and why they're on the run. I'll sign whatever papers you need."

As director, Beth had the leverage to make things happen that were outside the standard operating manual. He was counting on the fact that she was inclined to bend the rules if she thought it would benefit her kids.

"The only way you could keep them is if you became their temporary foster parent. That's not as easy as signing your name on the dotted line."

"What do I have to do?"

"Fill out an application. Attend orientation. Go through the certification process."

"I get it. Training classes, background checks, health screening, and a home study. I had a client once who wanted to adopt. I imagine it's a very similar process. How long will it take?"

"Four to eight weeks."

"We don't have that much time. I have a feeling the minute you take custody of these kids, they're going to run. I think housing them here on the ranch will keep them safe for a while."

"I could probably push the process along. You're certainly qualified. And your background check won't be a problem." She paused. "This could turn out to be not so temporary. Are you prepared for that?"

Good question. He'd left Seattle to start a new life, one that had nothing to do with what he'd left behind, but here he was, getting involved.

What other choice did he have?

Thinking he was loco, but also thinking of Jane and the bit of childhood she'd revealed to him, he made his decision fast. "Yes."

"Are you sure?"

"I am." In his mind's eye, Chase looked into a pair of inscrutable blue eyes that had seen more of the dark side of humanity than they should have, and hoped he was doing the right thing. "I'll have help."

"I'll need fingerprints to see if the kids are in the database."

He figured as much, but wasn't sure Bobby would be keen on cooperating. It didn't matter. There were ways. "I'll get them."

"Okay, then. I'll email the application form. Fill it out and send it to me as soon as you can."

After hanging up, he went to the kitchen to refill his coffee. When he returned to his office, the application was waiting for him.

Wondering if he'd bitten off more than he could chew, he completed the form, hesitating only briefly before hitting the send button.

~ * ~

A week into her enforced sojourn on Russell's ranch, Jane woke before dawn, restless and unable to stay in bed a moment longer. Despite hammering and painting her way through the outbuildings until she was so weary, anyone in their right mind would think she'd fall face first into bed and sleep without dreaming. She climbed out of bed with more on her mind than when she'd gone to bed.

Being raised in the orphanage had taught her a thing or two. One of them was that very few older children were ever fostered or adopted. There were probably statistics. She'd never bothered with them since she wasn't one of the lucky ones.

Abby was cute. She stood a chance of being picked up by loving parents. Bobby, on the other hand, had as much chance of that as a raindrop had of lasting more than a second in Hell.

She didn't for a minute question whether the kids came from a stable home. Once on your own, always on your own, was Jane's experience.

When she was younger, she'd envied the kids who, one way or the other, found families. But even then, she knew there was something about *her* that prospective parents didn't find appealing. She smirked, thinking she was more like Bobby than Abby. She liked to walk on the wild side. A rebel from the get-go. Okay, to call a spade a spade—she was defiant.

Her chances of being taken in by a normal, loving family had been zip. Nada. A big fat zero. Bobby had the same chance. She had to do something about that.

An idea she couldn't get rid of lurked in the back of her mind. She went downstairs to make coffee strong enough to grow hair where it wasn't wanted and, finding it already made, poured a cup. Bless Russell for liking his brew strong. She followed the faint light to his office.

He hunched over the keyboard, his overlong waves of hair

brushing his collar, begging her itchy fingers to resume their exploration. His strong jaw was locked in fierce concentration on the screen in front of him. The shadow of a mustache and beard he hadn't removed that morning had her clamping down on the sudden blast of desire to see if he could be enticed into another round of foreplay.

The irony didn't escape her. She'd come to the ranch to, with this man's help, dig at the roots of her problems. Instead, she was about to champion two kids who meant nothing to her.

She tapped her knuckle on the door jam. Russell looked up, then leaned back in his chair.

Pulling up a seat, she sank into it. "You look like you've been at it awhile."

"Couldn't sleep. Too much to do." He scrubbed his face with one strong, male hand.

She'd have to proceed with caution to get him to buy into her scheme. "What are you working on?"

He shrugged. "Checking a national register for missing children to see if Bobby or Abby are on it."

She nodded. Too many kids went missing each year. What would happen to these two if they left Russell's care?

Jane wasn't good at the subtle approach, but before she could come up with an opening, the man claiming more than half of her attention leaned forward on his elbows, his admirable intensity focused completely on her. "Tell me about Madrid."

They had more important things to talk about. Like making a future for Bobby and Abby on the ranch.

She sighed heartily. "I'd been in Madrid a year when I literally ran into Linus in the local bazaar. Or, he ran into me. He was living on the streets, panhandling for food."

"Why Linus?"

"I couldn't pronounce his real name. It sounded a little like Linus, and he reminded me of the Peanuts character."

Finding it difficult to go on, Jane jumped up from the chair and paced abruptly to the window. She stared out into the ranch yard, but that wasn't what she saw. Instead, it was the colorful booths of a Madrid bazaar on market day and a boy trying to stay alive the only way he knew how.

If not for Sister Mary Margaret and an orphanage in another country, that boy could have been her.

"I tried to find a local home for him. It never lasted long, and then he would disappear for a day, sometimes a week at a time, but he always came back. I thought we'd become fam—" she gulped in a breath and frowned. "It doesn't matter what I thought."

Her attention locked on that last day, she felt rather than saw Russell join her at the window.

"It started like any other day. Warm. The city was waking up with its usual bustle. Linus hadn't been around for close to two weeks. I was in my office trying to figure out where he could be when we got word unauthorized intruders had made it onto the grounds."

"How?"

"Later, we found out they dug a tunnel into the basement of one of the embassy buildings."

"What happened next?"

"Linus was one of them." She still couldn't believe it. "He was just a kid. And…and, my friend."

An arm slipped around her shoulders, offering a comfort she was tempted to accept but knew she didn't deserve.

Finally, the horror of a boy she cared about blowing himself to bits and a building falling on her head faded. Sunlight glinted off newly whitewashed outbuildings. Beside her, a concerned, generous man didn't want her to hurt anymore. She swung to face him.

Eyes full of compassion, he said gruffly, "That's what terrorists do. They take what's good in this world and destroy it."

Jane dropped her chin to her chest. "I know."

"You can't let them win by throwing your life away."

"I know!" She snapped, her tender feelings toward the man turning to dust.

"What are you doing, then?"

She struggled in silence for a long moment as a startling thought raced through her mind. *I'm not my mother. I won't abandon a kid when I'm all they have to look after them.*

Fast on the heels of that came the searing guilt she'd been living with. She hadn't done a bang-up job of looking after Linus. She put the two thoughts away to be examined when her emotions weren't reeling.

Taking a fortifying drag of country air, she raised her chin. "What are you going to do with Bobby and Abby?"

Russell's brows quirked up. "I've got a friend at the county working on it."

"You could keep them here. They like you. And you would keep them safe." She was convinced of it.

His arm dropped from her shoulder. "I've applied to be their foster parent. Temporarily anyway, until we…you…figure out who they are and where they came from."

For a brief moment, the briefest one ever, she missed his warm touch. "Temporary? If Sister Mary Margaret hadn't taken me in when I was a baby, who knows where I'd be now? If I'd done a better job of looking after Linus, maybe things

102

would have turned out differently in Madrid. I don't want anything bad to happen to Bobby and Abby."

Jane relaxed the fists her hands had made. Coming at Russell with all the anger sitting on her chest wouldn't get a stable home for the children. "They deserve more than a temporary parent. You'd be doing a good thing."

"That may not be possible. Their parents are probably looking for them right now."

With one hand, she waved his objection aside. "Happy kids don't run just for the heck of it." Her gaze drifted back to the view out the window. She spoke softly, mostly to herself. "You have the perfect home for them here."

"I can't make any promises about where Bobby and Abby will end up, but I promise I won't let anything bad happen to them."

He took her hand, palm to palm, intertwining their fingers. She felt the connection clear to the ruins of her defenses. Sometime during their exchange, her walls had crumbled, leaving her defenseless against the man turning her knees weak.

When he squeezed her hand, arousal re-ignited. Lust didn't even begin to describe the feeling nipping at her heels.

It was bigger. Deeper. Burned in her chest. She didn't have a name for it and would be afraid to whisper it if she did.

"I need your help. Discovering Abby's name so quickly was a lucky start, but if I'm going to be any use to them, I need to know more."

Russell needed her.

Jane hadn't been needed or needed anyone herself in a long while. But with his sharp gaze capturing hers, seeing deeper than she'd ever allowed anyone else to, as simple as that, they became cohorts. Not a counselor and his patient. But a man and woman united in their determination to protect two lost kids.

She pulled her hand free from his and wrapped her arms around her stomach. This was not what she'd signed on for when she'd first arrived and persuaded him to help her. On the other hand, she couldn't walk away when there might be something she could do that would make a difference.

Russell knew that. She knew it. There was no point in putting up a fight.

I'm not my mother.

"All right, I'll help."

TEN

Later that day, Chase settled on the top step of the porch to watch Jane give Abby a slow, rumbling ride around the ranch yard. He pulled on the bill of his baseball cap to block out the bright afternoon sunlight. Bobby was perched on the top rail of the corral.

He frowned. That morning, he'd come so close to saying the hell with his professionalism and seeing just what it would take to make the pretty warrior woman come apart in his arms.

His good judgment had taken a vacation, just like it had with Nate, and he'd come that close to making a mess of the job his uncle had given him.

It was irritating to admit, but it felt good to be working again. Matt was right about that. It was just unfortunate that he didn't seem to be able to control his physical reaction to the spunky lady.

The more he found out what made her tick, the more under her spell he fell. He didn't like being enthralled, but the question was, what was he going to do about it?

"Go again," Abby squealed gleefully.

Jane laughed, a rare occurrence. Abby giggled with her. Chase's stomach took a hard tumble.

It was a side of the tough woman he didn't need to see. The instant clench of need was so strong that it took all his willpower to stay sitting where he was, rather than taking Abby's place and insisting Jane take the road back to the lake where he'd last tasted her.

He forced the image from his mind. He couldn't keep thinking of her that way. She needed his professional expertise, not this randy teenager's reaction to the prettiest girl in school.

They had a deal. He would counsel. She would cooperate by participating in his idea of therapeutic counseling.

He'd introduce her to impulse control, anger management, and selective social skills. She'd return to her former life as emotionally healthy as it was possible to get during her thirty days with him.

There could be nothing more to their relationship than that.

Jane stopped the motorcycle in front of Bobby. Before Abby's feet hit the dirt, the little girl was chattering like a magpie. "Bobby, did you see me? Can I go again?"

"It's my turn, brat," grumbled the teen in good spirits as he climbed down from the corral and then removed his sister's helmet.

Gus sat down. "I ran into Maxi in town this morning." His foreman liked having his morning coffee at one of the local cafes in Lone Pine. "She's agreed to sell ya four horses."

Chase tore his gaze away from Jane. If he could occupy himself with something besides how hot she looked carting two lost kids around on a big, bad Harley, maybe she would stop taking up so much space in his mind. "How did you talk her into that?"

"Told her they was for the children."

"Uh-huh." From what Chase had seen of his crusty neighbor, it would take more than that to get her to change her mind. "Just like that, she decided to fraternize with the city slicker?"

A red stain blotched Gus' cheeks. Abby skipped over, plopped down on Chase's other side, and leaned against his arm. His handyman stuttered, "I, uh… promised to take her to the Lone Pine Rodeo Dance."

"You don't have to do that."

"It's all right, I was going anyway," Gus muttered, staring at his boots, then slapped the battered hat he held by the brim on his head. "Got work to do. She'll be here in half an hour."

The old man hadn't taken many steps before he spun around. "Maybe you should think about taking Miss Jane."

Chase found Jane's laughing gaze across the ranch yard. She made quite a picture tooling around his drive with Bobby hanging on behind her.

His pulse leaped. *Then again, maybe I shouldn't.*

~ * ~

Three days later, Jane woke to the smell of strong, potent coffee, the heady aroma reminding her of the man who'd pushed them all to get ready for this camping trip he insisted they take into the hill country above the ranch.

She rolled out of her sleeping bag almost fully clothed. After pulling on her boots and throwing a large camp shirt over her tank, she gratefully accepted the mug of coffee Russell placed in her hands before retreating with his cup to the other side of the fire.

He studied her over the steaming drink. "Better?" The low

growl in his voice was seductive, filled with the edges of sleep not completely gone.

"Yes. Thanks." An unexpected desire to know what it would feel like to snuggle up next to him in front of the day's first fire snuck up, cracking her voice.

It didn't take additional couch time to figure out, more than the battle over her mental health waged between them. She'd been ignoring the truth for days.

Admit it, Donovan. You like the guy. You like him a lot.

She wasn't going to admit anything of the sort. She had another purpose for him. His job was to untangle her mind, not get tangled up in the sheets with her, no matter how delicious that sounded.

In the first months after being buried alive under the rubble of what was left of the basement where she'd found Linus and the other two intruders, her memory of what had happened those last minutes was spotty at best. The missing pieces were there; she could feel them, but they remained just beyond her reach.

At first, she'd thought she'd been betrayed by the boy she'd recklessly grown to care about. But she'd thought about it long and hard, and the truth was worse than that. *She* was the one who'd betrayed him.

By leaving him vulnerable and unprotected, she'd given unscrupulous snakes a chance to take advantage of both their weaknesses. Until she could come to terms with that, she was afraid she had no chance of putting her life back together.

She shivered. When the edges of her vision cleared, Russell was squatting in front of her, adding his warmth to the fire's. "What is it?"

That's when it hit her—the reason for her restless dreams

during the night. She didn't want to stay out in the cold, alone in her frozen past any longer. Not when this strong, astute man looked at her like he wanted to fight off all contenders to be the one to slay her dragon.

"Jane?"

"I… I'm fine. Really," she lied.

On the one hand, she wanted to go home to Paris Island. On the other, there were these unexplainable… feelings … for Russell she found it almost impossible to ignore and was discovering that she didn't want to.

"I don't believe you."

Taking her coffee cup from her, he captured her hands. Just his touch locked the breath in her chest, leaving her unable to escape the raw desire exploding in her belly.

This couldn't be good. It was crazy. All of a sudden, she was wondering what would happen if she didn't return to her other life. Not because she didn't get well, but because there was a possibility, albeit a very minute one, that she'd accidentally stumbled on a dream she'd discarded long ago.

Stunned, she went still. She wasn't looking for happy-ever-after. Nor did she lead the kind of life conducive to finding it. But, if she thought there was one chance in hell, she could jump the hurdles and make a military marriage—_okay,_ any marriage—work, wouldn't it be worth checking out the man who might make it last longer than the time it took to decide something else was more important than she was?

Jane mentally shook herself free of the startling idea. She wasn't an innocent. She'd been to more than one dance. None had lasted longer than the ride home and a smattering of dates after.

Russell wasn't her dream guy. He couldn't be.

"I shouldn't want you, but I do," the man in question ground out, frustration firming his jaw.

Jane grabbed the edges of her vaporizing will and held on for dear life. "What if I don't want you?"

Another lie. She was positive he would have believed it if she'd done a better job of keeping the breathlessness out of her voice.

His frown evaporated into a cocky grin. "You're so surprising," he murmured, raising her hand to his lips. He nipped her knuckles, causing spiraling heat to flare in her belly.

Rational thought deserted her, except for one teeny, tiny voice. *What's wrong with taking a little pleasure when it's offered?*

Just this once, she wished she could give in and let this man's quiet strength defeat her monsters for her. After all, Marines were trained from day one to be team players.

She cleared her throat, warning him, "I don't stay in one place long, and no matter what happens, I'll go."

With his free hand, he tucked a strand of hair behind her ear. "And I'll stay."

Visions of them intertwined in a big bed had her greedy for the real thing. How many rules would they break?

It turned out she didn't care. She was more than willing to toss the rule book out.

"Miss Jane?" Jane blinked at the sleepy voice at her elbow. "I have to go."

Shaken at how much she wanted Russell's strong hands exploring her intimate places, and even more by how desperate she was to feel something besides the cold emptiness she'd been carrying around for so long, she scrambled to her feet.

Taking hold of Abby's hand, she turned her back on the best offer she'd had in years. "Okay, let's go."

Congratulating herself for sidestepping a very close call, she guided the little girl to an outhouse just beyond the camp. They passed Bobby, still sleeping, buried up to his ears in his sleeping bag, his wild stock of brown hair poking out at unruly angles.

She had work to do, besides panting over her sexy therapist. Discovering the kids' real identities was her top priority.

Jane whispered a little prayer to the big guy upstairs that a few well-placed questions would quickly elicit the information Russell required, thereby unlocking the chains that bound her to the man and his delightful ranch.

Starting now. "How did you sleep last night?"

"Okay." A small, slender hand slapped over a yawn. When they got to the square, well-kept facility, the little girl gave Jane a nervous look. "I can go in by myself."

Abby didn't know they'd already discovered she wasn't the boy she was pretending to be.

"Sure." She sat on a nearby boulder and waited. When the little girl came out a few minutes later, they crossed the dirt lane to a spigot sticking up out of the ground and washed their hands. The water ran cold.

"Do you like being on the ranch?"

"It's fun," Abby said, like fun didn't often come her way. Memories of her lonely childhood crowded out the list Jane was compiling in her mind of all the reasons why she shouldn't work in a *very* personal session with the man back at the campsite.

"You know you can trust me, right? 'Cause I know your name's not Pete Jones."

Abby's eyes went round with sudden wariness. "Bobby says we can't trust anyone. Not even Gol-"

The scared look on the kid's sweet face cut deep into Jane's heart. Trust was a slippery slope. One that could easily be used against you. She'd learned that the hard way and wished she didn't have to give these kids the same lesson. But what choice did she have? Their safety had to come first.

"I can help. Mr. Russell wants to help, too. Can't you at least tell me your first name?"

Abby shook her head vigorously.

"Alright. But, if you change your mind—" At least she'd sown a seed. "Come on. Let's see about breakfast."

Abby tucked her little hand into Jane's. A startling picture of coming home to her very own family each night pounced, catching her in its trap. What would it be like to have a precious little girl like this one to love and treasure?

It was frightening that wherever Bobby and Abby's mother was, the woman didn't have a clue, or worse, didn't care what had happened to her children. Jane had always dismissed the idea that she could one day have a daughter, certain she wouldn't make a good mom. Her own mother had never won any mom-of-the-year awards.

If, however, by some precarious quirk of fate, she found herself with just such a daughter? By god, she would do better than both of them. Never would she leave her child to the fickle whim of strangers.

Abby hopped a few steps. "Can I cook eggs?"

"You can help."

"Miss Jane?"

A sharp tug jerked her away from planning what her next move would be in uncovering the kids' identities. Abby stopped them by a large tree lying on the ground. Using their joined hands for balance, she climbed onto the fallen trunk, stared at Jane, then appearing to make up her mind that it was okay to trust this stranger she'd only known for a short while, nodded. "My name is Abby."

Jane faked surprise. "You're a girl?"

Her eyes round, the child nodded.

"Abby's a much prettier name than Pete. Thank you for telling me." She wanted to do a victory dance, but instead, she resumed walking.

Madrid wasn't going to repeat itself, not if she had anything to say about it. If nothing else good came of her stay on Russell's ranch, this sweet little girl was going to end up in a safe place.

~ * ~

Chase couldn't keep his eyes off Jane as she hovered protectively over his littlest surprise border. Together, they made breakfast, the Marine quietly instructing Abby over a banked campfire.

Dressed in jeans, her usual tank, and an oversized blue shirt that matched her eyes, with her hair falling haphazardly around her face, this woman was a far cry from the tense soldier who'd shown up at his ranch a week and a half ago.

Her recovery plan called for recreational activities to help reintroduce her to a normal life. A camping trip was the most *normal activity* he'd been able to come up with.

Admittedly, most people didn't go camping on horseback, but with this little trip in mind, he'd begun researching equine-assisted therapy for post-traumatic stress disorders in returning veterans. He'd wanted to find out if the modality would help the woman firing off his senses as if there could be no tomorrow without her, and he'd been pleasantly surprised by how much information there was on the net.

A campground that allowed horses was close enough to get to by way of a short ride. Hoping to reach Jane in this somewhat unconventional way, he'd worked the horses into her treatment plan.

But, he couldn't do it alone, so he'd enlisted Gus' help and spent the days since Maxine delivered the animals, giving riding lessons—lessons the Marine, with her usual endurance, discipline, and intelligence, had passed with flying colors.

He'd introduced all three to the beasts and made them spend hours grooming and getting to know the personalities of their respective mounts. All the while, thinking...

Thinking what? He could be more than Jane's therapist? That she somehow fit his idea of the perfect woman?

Her arrogant, brooding edginess should have been a solid put-off. He liked his woman soft, feminine, and easy on the senses. The Marine was not that. Unfortunately, her courage and headstrong determination were sexier than any traditional female archetype he'd thought, before meeting her, was the kind of woman he might someday marry.

She was tough as nails; her emotions locked up where no one could get to them. But when she opened up enough to allow Abby and Bobby inside her defensive walls, how could he resist the attraction?

Before she'd shown up, his life had been organized exactly the way he wanted. Quiet. Uneventful. Without undue responsibility. Then, she'd arrived on his doorstep and all but dragged him back into the profession he'd given up.

Inexplicably, he wanted more. Something elusive he couldn't quite put his finger on.

After failing his brother, Chase had been afraid to be responsible for anyone else and their mental health. Thanks to Jane, whether he ever went back into private practice or not, she'd forced him to face what was done and then begin to trust himself to do the right thing. If he didn't accept the truth of that, how could he expect her to?

Jane's delighted laughter at Abby's attempt to cook shot straight to his besieged heart.

"Here's your breakfast." Abby brought him a plate. It was piled high with potatoes, scrambled eggs, and fried bread. She fairly danced in her excitement. "I helped cook it."

"I saw that." He took the plate from the child and couldn't help smiling as she raced, as fast as her cast would let her, back to Jane to get her food.

They brought their plates to the half-moon arrangement of logs he'd set up. A still yawning Bobby joined them.

It took two to tango—his mother's saying, not his. Chase pushed away the image of him and Jane learning each other's moves.

If this little adventure worked, she'd be gone from his life and back in the one she'd almost destroyed.

Abby plunked down next to Jane, barely giving the smiling woman elbow room. With one exploring finger, she tentatively touched the bracelet he'd never seen the Marine without. "I like your bracelet."

The flat, hammered piece of metal on a long, narrow knotted strip of worn leather wound around her wrist multiple times as though it'd originally been made to be a necklace.

Jane looked down and froze. Her eyes glazed over. Sweat beaded on her forehead. Moving fast, Chase swore, barely saving her plate from falling to the ground. Squatting in front of her, he placed it on the log beside her.

A flashback. Not uncommon in returning vets. Having no

rhyme or reason, anything could set them off.

He cupped her knee so she would know he was there and that he cared. Perhaps more than he should—not in a you're-my-client, I'm-your-therapist kind of way.

"It's okay. You're safe."

But was he?

ELEVEN

"What's wrong with Miss Jane?" Abby's voice shook. "Bobby, get Jane a blanket." Chase took both her fists, rubbing his thumbs urgently over her white knuckles.

Behind him, the horses stomped, blowing air out of their nostrils. She blinked, then blinked again. He knew only one way to break the flashback's hold on her. Practical, reassuring words to remind her where she was.

"Jane, you're having a flashback. You're safe at the campground. I've got a hike planned for later, but first, we'll finish eating and take care of the horses. You and…Pete made a fine breakfast this morning."

Bobby quickly returned, a blanket balled up in his arms. "What do you want me to do with it?"

"Wrap her in it. Pete, can you help? Stay close to her."

Chase had to give the kids credit. Though they looked scared, they didn't panic.

After dragging the blanket around Jane's shoulders, Pete...
Abby leaned against the Marine's arm. Bobby closely guarded
her other side.

"Come back, Jane. You can do it."

A shudder racked her stiff body. She briefly met his gaze,
then leaned forward and laid her forehead against his galloping
heartbeat. Her hands shook. He almost did, too.

He slipped his arms around her in a crushing hold that
threatened never to let go. Silky hair brushed his chin. The
tremor that snaked through her stiff body nearly undid him.
Never had he been so gut-wrenching affected by the sight of
one of his patients experiencing a side effect of their time on
the battlefield.

"I can't go back, can I?" Her voice was a broken whisper.

He knew exactly what she was asking, and he ached for
her. Too much to keep his vaulted objectivity. He rushed to
reassure her with what he hoped was the truth. "You can."

"The flashbacks are getting worse." Her shoulders slumped.

"That's because you're starting to heal."

"I don't want to put my buddies in jeopardy."

For the first time, she sounded defeated. Chase tightened his
arms around her. He couldn't leave the courageous lady alone
in that dark place. Rashly, he told her, "You won't. I promise."

He felt the sharp intake of her breath as though he were the
one fighting for air. She raised her head, looking at him so full
of self-doubt, it cut deep into his heart.

"How can you know that?"

He took her by the shoulders. "We'll give you the tools you
need to fight your way back."

To his surprise, he *wanted* her to lean on him, take what
strength she could from him. Never had he needed to help

a patient overcome their demons the way he did with this inspiring woman. It brought him up short.

She studied him for a long moment, the panic and doubt gripping her lithe body starting to recede. "What do I have to do?"

He didn't want to leave her, but he motioned for her to stay where she was. Taking several searching steps toward the fire, Chase found what he was looking for.

When he returned, her gorgeous blues had cleared of the horrific images he was sure were sharper than the day she'd gone through the terrifying events. His stoic Marine was back, which could be a good or bad thing, depending on how she reacted to his next suggestion.

It was a little unorthodox out here in the middle of ranching wilderness, and with the kids looking on, but he had to take a shot while she was willing to give anything a try.

She'd angled an arm around Abby. He handed her the slender stick he'd picked up. "Draw a picture of Linus in the dirt here."

She frowned. "I can't."

"You can." He squatted in front of her, leaving room between them for the drawing.

For a long second, all he could see was a beautiful woman who was hurt beyond anything he could imagine. All he wanted to do was take her in his arms and make it all better.

He cleared his throat. "Tell us about Linus while you draw."

Bobby hovered nearby, his eyes locked on her face, his hands stuffed in his pants pockets. Abby wiggled into a comfortable position on Jane's lap.

The lady had no idea how much the kids had grown to care about her. How much *he* cared about her.

"What if I have another flashback?"

She was breathtaking. A stubborn survivor. The bravest woman he'd ever met. And, he was fast on his way to being in way over his head.

Before he could make sense out of it all, he had to get her to talk her way out of the foxhole she'd dug herself into. "Concentrate on where you are, the sounds you hear. The campground. The horses. The campfire. Making breakfast with friends. Think about how fresh the air smells. How the birds sound. Make a mantra of it. You're safe, and we're right here with you."

She nodded, took a deep breath, and then squeezed Abby. "I'm sorry I scared you. Linus was my friend. He gave the bracelet to me for my last birthday."

She leaned over, keeping the little girl in place on her lap, and began sketching in the dirt.

Shaken by the depth of his feelings, Chase fought for his lost objectivity, struggling to sort his feelings out. How could he see her as just another client when the crack in her tough shell and her dauntless spirit took the wind right out of his sails?

Determined to play his part, he focused on the drawing emerging on the dirt palette. It was a basic stick drawing, with hair sticking straight out from a long oval head.

Jane was talking, more to herself than her audience. "Linus was ten when I first met him. By then, he'd already been living on the streets of Madrid for two years."

Bobby edged closer. "Spain?"

She nodded. "His favorite food was goat cheese and olives. That day, I gave him his first chocolate bar. After that, I always had to have one in my pocket."

She added a baggy tunic and pants, with bare feet sticking out of the wide pant legs.

120

Abby shivered in her lap. "Something bad happened to him, didn't it?"

"He was killed." Jane's gaze jerked up to his, and he saw the instant she figured it out.

It was terrorists who'd drugged the boy and turned him into a suicide bomber, not a lack of diligence on her part. He watched her fight the stark realization and had to catch himself before he fell irrevocably into a situation he couldn't walk away from.

She dropped the stick and rubbed the back of her hand across her eyes, breaking their tenuous cord.

"You're okay," Abby said in her more adult than little girl way, and wrapped too-thin arms around Jane's neck in silent comfort.

When she drew back, her tiny hand tangled in the chain just visible above the neck of Jane's tee. Dog tags tumbled free.

Jane's gaze snapped back to him, seeking answers. Answers she would only find inside herself. When he slowly nodded, the tension she'd carried like a shroud from the moment she arrived on his doorstep eased from the depths of her eyes.

It turned to something else between them. Something light and—not that he'd experienced it before to know exactly what it was—magical.

Careful, Russell.

Without breaking their simmering connection, she spoke to Abby, "Yes, I believe I am going to be okay."

Bobby stared at the dog tags. "You're a soldier?"

She looked over at the boy. "Yes."

"A Marine?"

"That's right."

A look passed between the kids. When Bobby turned back

to Jane, unconscious pride lifted his chin. "Our father is a Marine."

"He is? Where's he stationed?"

"I don't know." The kid squared his shoulders. "Could you help us find him?"

"It's possible. What's his name?"

Chase could see the wheels turning in Jane's head. He'd bet the ranch she was thinking the same thing he was.

Bobby glanced at his sister and hesitated.

"You should tell her."

He shrugged one shoulder. "Jack Malone. Sergeant Jack Malone."

"Not Jones?"

Bobby kicked at the dirt and remained silent.

"Okay. What about your mother? Where's she?"

Pressing his lips into a thin line, the teenager crossed his arms over his scrawny chest. Watching them go toe to toe gave Chase some insight into what it would be like if she were still around when the kid hit seventeen.

He went motionless at the thought before grabbing fleeing reality. Jane would be leaving. Soon, if how well she'd recovered from this flashback was anything to go by.

Her calculated shrug had his pulse lurching. "I guess you don't have to tell me if you don't want to."

"She was killed in a car accident."

Easy enough to verify. Chase waited, his heart warming as he watched the remarkable woman put her talents to good use.

"I'll ask around about your dad, but only on one condition."

Bobby pushed his hands deep into his pants pockets. "What condition?"

ELEVEN

"Tell us your name."

Abby slapped a hand across her mouth. Bobby pinned her with a disgusted look. "You told, didn't you?"

Dropping her gaze in abject misery to her shoes, the little girl nodded.

Jane stood, carrying Abby with her, as if that alone would offer protection against a brother's anger. Chase took a hard punch at the sight. She was just beginning to believe it, but the woman emerging? She was going to be all right.

Right then, he lost the fight to stay objective, to keep himself aloof from her spell. There was nothing he could do but cross his fingers and hope he hadn't taken the biggest fall of his life.

Throwing his shoulders back and stretching to his full height, Bobby, or whoever he was, faced them head-on. "My name is Zach. Zach Malone."

~ * ~

For the first time in a long time, Jane felt good. Strong. Like she could take on the skeletons in her closet and win.

Thanks to Chase. She thought of him that way now. In her mind, where her restraints had been broken, and the fearless Jane Donovan she used to be had been set free.

And she knew one thing. She was going to have to fire him. Soon. Because he couldn't be her therapist any longer. Not when what she wanted from him had nothing to do with behavior or cognitive therapy.

She wasn't free of Madrid, but she was closer than she'd been since her arrival on the ranch. When she'd followed his voice back from the dark place the flashback had taken her, he'd promised to be there for her.

What she wanted from Chase Russell was a little play therapy. Oh, not children's games. Adult, hot, sweaty games that involved bare skin, heavy breathing, and intertwined bodies.

A little voice poked her. Was she the classic patient falling for her therapist? Did it matter? Not really. She'd be leaving soon. With the Doc's blessing.

But before she ran him to ground, she had a couple of kids to take care of. Waiting patiently, she listened for the click of Zach and Abby's bedroom door, then moved up the stairs on silent feet until she was close enough to hear the murmur of their voices. It probably wasn't fair to eavesdrop on their conversation, but she'd given up playing fair in Madrid.

Zach wanted her to find his father. If the man could be found, she would.

"You lied." Abby's voice was almost too quiet to hear through the door. Jane leaned closer.

"Don't worry about it."

There was a short silence. "What if they find out?"

"They won't."

Lied? Of course he did, but about what?

"Zach?"

"Shh."

"Do you think Miss Jane can find Pop?"

"Maybe."

"Should we tell her he flies helicopters?"

"Don't be a worrywart. I'll tell her at dinner."

Jane eased away. In her room, she flipped open her cell and dialed. "Johnson? Donovan here. I need a favor."

"What can I do for you, Ma'am?"

No hesitation. That was the Corps for you.

"I need you to find a Jack Malone. He could be assigned to an Air Wing."

"Sure thing. Anything specific you're looking for?"

"His current duty station and intel on his family—wife, two kids."

The click of Johnson's computer keys brought back good memories. Jane welcomed them, moved to the window to stare at the high desert landscape.

She wondered if the Malones' marriage had ended in divorce. It wasn't uncommon in the military. It took a tough spouse to stay married to a soldier. Which was one of the reasons, besides never finding the right guy, why she hadn't gone down that road herself. When it didn't work, it was often the children who paid the biggest price.

"I can give you his location. I'll have to get back to you on the rest."

Johnson was a whiz kid on the computer. If anyone could get answers, it would be the junior Marine.

It took longer than Jane expected for him to locate Malone's personnel records. The news wasn't good.

Sighing heavily, she disconnected the call. It wasn't the first time she'd delivered bad news, nor would it be the last. It was just that after the way they'd stood by her at the campsite, the kids deserved more than finding out their dream of finding their father was a dead end.

She found them in the kitchen. Chase was at the stove, fixing dinner. The smell of sizzling hamburgers and fried potatoes saturated the air. Gus and Zach were starting up a game of checkers.

Chase laughed at something Abby said, and just for a moment, Jane didn't want to deliver the news that would shatter this cozy picture. The chatter died as they looked at her expectantly.

There was no way to soften the blow, so Jane squared her

shoulders and gave it to them straight. "I talked to my Corporal back at the base. Six months ago, Captain Jack Malone was killed when his helicopter went down in Afghanistan. He's survived by his ex-wife and two children."

Matching shocked expressions tore at her heart. They were too young and innocent to be dealt this blow. A feeling of kinship caught her breath. She softened her voice. "I'm so sorry."

"He's dead," Zach muttered, shock spreading across his young face. His shoulders dropped. Lips trembled before he pressed them firmly together.

Fat tears welled up in Abby's eyes as she ran as best she could to throw her arms around her brother's neck.

Gus swore under his breath.

Jane set her jaw, refusing to look at Chase. "Do you have any other relatives? An aunt or uncle?"

"There's no one." Zach's chin dipped to the top of his sister's head.

They were all alone now. She knew what that felt like. Not sure what else to do, she moved to grab them and offer what comfort she could. Chase beat her to it, placing a steady hand on their shoulders.

"Zach, what are we going to do?" A watery hiccup escaped Abby as she looked up with anxious eyes at her brother. Tears that wrenched Jane's gut slid down the little girl's face.

She'd meant to stay uninvolved, keep her side of the bargain with Zach, nothing more, but how could she make this right for them? She had nothing to offer. She wasn't one of those women who could skillfully pull maternal sympathy out of her over-large handbag, or who innately knew how to make a child feel better when their world was crashing at their feet.

Damn it, she couldn't even keep her own world from falling apart.

"You'll stay here with me." With those five precious words, Chase did what she couldn't. He rode to the rescue, grabbed hold of two lost lives, and brought them out of the storm to safety.

Jane's panic button went off, and not in a post-traumatic-I'm-having-a-panic-attack way either. Struck by an overpowering urge to run, fast and as far away as she could get, she wondered if she'd just witnessed one of those miracles Sister Mary Margaret had always talked about; the ones Jane didn't believe in at all.

Before she'd joined the Corps, she'd longed for just such a family. She'd thought she'd found it within the community of Marines, but standing here watching the three of them, she realized that elusive dream of having her own family, a mom and dad who loved their children more than anything else. It was dangling right in front of her nose.

Now that she looked back on her time with Linus in Madrid, she realized that was exactly what she'd tried to do with him. Make a family. She hadn't been aware of it until just this minute, and she'd gone about it all wrong, but—

Was this the missing piece all along? Chase and these two kids who needed him, and maybe her too?

She tromped solidly on the ridiculous notion that with her lack of experience in this particular area, she would ever qualify to be part of a normal family. Despite the lockdown she forced on her emotions, the old yearnings surfaced.

Chase's gaze collided with hers, included her, and offered safe harbor.

She stood at a crossroads. To the right was the life she knew, the one she was desperate to return to. To the left was quite possibly everything she'd never allowed herself to dream of. A family of her very own. A home filled with warmth and laughter. A lifetime snuggled up in the arms of that one special man who made a girl's heart beat like thunder.

But Jane knew fairy tales did not come true. At least not for her.

Zach and Abby and Gus, they belonged here on this ranch. Her life was the Marine Corps, three thousand miles away.

Regret stole into her heart. The kids needed Chase much more than she did. She'd done a good thing. Managed to find a bit of redemption by playing a small role in helping to keep them safe. She would have to be content with that.

It was safer that way. Much safer than watching Chase maneuver the kids away from their shock.

"There's going to be a rodeo with a barbecue and dance in Lone Pine tomorrow. How about we all go?"

Chase wrapped her in an illusion she had to reject.

"I guess." The misery in Zach's sunken shoulders was mirrored in his sister's downturned mouth. It was enough to rattle Jane's resolve.

Chase turned the suffering kids so he could squat in front of them. "I'm sorry about your Dad. It's not what we'd hoped to find. If it's okay, I have a friend who can make it possible for you to stay here as long as you want."

Zach's gaze snapped up from the fists he'd made in his lap.

If the Corps didn't already have dibs on her, Jane would have snatched the man by his lapels, begging him to let her stay and become a part of this little family he was gathering to his heart.

Abby came up with her own solution and scared the crap out of Jane. "You and Miss Jane could adopt us."

Chase's eyes swiveled in her direction, causing her heart to tumble over the cliff she teetered on. "I was thinking more along the lines of being your foster parent, but adoption's an option, too."

In a heartbeat, the emotional distance she'd worked so hard to maintain evaporated. Chase Russell was something else. What was he going to do? Take in every stray adult and child that came his way?

She'd been scheming for him to keep the kids permanently, but adoption hadn't crossed her mind. She didn't dare hope for something that lasting for Zach and Abby.

She'd never forgotten what it felt like to have her hopes of a real family dashed against the realities of life. Surprising anticipation skimmed down her back at the questioning challenge springing at her from Chase's cinnamon eyes.

Did she have what it took to see this through? To do what she was suddenly afraid he wanted her to do?

She shook her head. She was leaving. Zach and Abby would be much better off if she quashed this insane idea right now.

When she opened her mouth to do just that, she couldn't find the words that would disappoint the two kids gazing at her with stark longing. Neither could she admit her growing feelings for the man staring at her as though he understood every inch of the struggle she was going through.

TWELVE

T he next day, after leaving Gus in the stockyard swapping tales with his cronies, Jane took in the view of Chase's backside as he found seats for them across from the announcer's booth, where they could easily see the riding events.

He was dressed casually in a blue T-shirt that showed off the well-defined muscles of his chest. Jeans sat low on his narrow hips, causing her to drool in the most unladylike manner. Sexy cowboy boots had her catching her breath, the image of tall, dark, and too cocky playing havoc with her desire to go home and forget the guy.

She'd spent a restless night circling her options, and she'd acknowledged some hard truths. She hoped Chase *could* adopt Zach and Abby, not just be their foster parent. Deep down inside, she wanted to be a part of what he was doing here on the ranch, but Scott's visit had shown her one thing.

She missed her life in the Corps. In that place, she knew who she was and what to expect. Her days there were measured and routine. There were no surprises.

A Marine through and through, she liked that about herself. Yes, she'd stumbled for a while, but she was getting a handle on that.

And these feelings roaming in her chest for Chase? They were too overwhelming; left her too unsettled.

With the sun hanging high in a clear blue sky, she sat beside him on the hard bleachers. She could smell anticipation in the air as the stands started to fill, and was just as thrilled as Abby when clowns, faces painted with a bright red smile on white faces, came into the ring. Even Zach dropped his discouraged air.

His amused gaze meeting hers over Abby's head, Chase slipped off his sunglasses, hanging them in the neck of his shirt.

When it came time to go, she would, but it couldn't hurt to finish up her leave by enjoying herself. With this amazing man. And with the kids. Could it?

"What are they doing?" Zach scooted to the edge of his seat, craning his neck to see the chute where a cowboy was carefully mounting a temperamental bull.

Chase cast her a speculative look that had Jane's mouth going dry as desert sand. She barely resisted fanning herself and was strangely disappointed when he took his eyes off her to answer Zach's question.

"This is the bull-riding event. Those cowboys over there are going to see who can stay on the longest."

"Look. The clown. He waved at me!" Abby squealed in delight.

One minute she was there, using the top rail to steady herself as she waved at the clown. The next, even as Jane reached for the back of her shorts to hang on to the excited child, Abby yelped, tumbling over the rail into the arena.

The same instant, a horn blared. Locking mechanisms clanked open on the gate that held the first bull and its rider captive. The crowd roared.

"Abby!" Her heart jumping to her throat, Jane threw herself over the railing. Caught at the waist, she hung upside down, barely keeping her feet planted while she reached down with both hands to grab the little girl.

Abby's eyes went round with terror. Furious hooves pounded at Jane's back. When she looked up, the clowns were shouting and waving their arms in an attempt to redirect the wild animal. Bucking his way in a cloud of spraying dust straight for them, his eyes blazing and his nostrils flaring, the animal paid no attention.

Terror lodged in her throat. "Abby! Grab my hands!"

Frantic to reach the frightened child before disaster struck in the form of a ton of angry bull, she scooted a little more onto the rail only to find herself perched precariously like a teeter-totter. Her heart thumping, all she could think of was preventing the animal from stomping Abby to death.

Stretching as far down as she could, she made one last grab for the child's outstretched hands. She hauled the child into her arms, but the law of gravity was against her, and they began a slow slide downward where she was sickly certain, within seconds, they would be trampled by maniacal hoofs.

She tried to curl her body around Abby.

Then strong hands grabbed the back of her jeans. Chase reached over her shoulder, plucked Abby out of her arms as though the girl were a light-weight sack of potatoes.

"Oh no, you don't." He plunked them both on the bench beside him to the wild applause of the spectators who'd witnessed the near catastrophe. "Didn't you girls read the signs? No playing in the arena with the animals."

The words were playful, but there was a steely look in Chase's eyes that shook Jane's control. His hands skimmed up and down her arms, waking a dangerous awareness she'd been trying desperately all day to ignore.

Beside her, Abby described her ordeal in delighted, blood-thirsty detail as though Zach hadn't been right there to witness the whole thing. "That bull was running right at me."

"How could I be so stupid?" Jane managed past the cold sweat chilling her in the midday heat. "She could have been killed."

"She's okay." His hands settled possessively at her shoulders. "You scared the shit...that was a courageous thing you did."

"Desperate is more like it." She drew in a steadying breath. It wasn't diving headfirst into an arena with an angry bull determined to stomp the life out of her that was giving her shivers now. It was the man looking at her as if he would be devastated if something terrible happened to her. "I was flat out afraid. If Abby had been hurt—"

Chase gently touched her face. "I thought Marines weren't afraid of anything."

For a long moment, Jane stared at him. Then, the words tumbled out. "I'm always afraid." She suppressed a shiver. "Afraid I won't be there when it matters the most, that I don't have what it takes to stick when things get tough."

Russell tugged her close enough to feel the heat from his body. "You're not your mother."

With a sigh of relief, she rested her forehead against his

shoulder. "No. I'm not."

~ * ~

Later, when night had closed in on them and the sight of Abby tumbling into the arena was beginning to fade, Jane settled at a table in the Thunder Room Bar. She rubbed the raw spot on her belly with her fingertips. When she caught sight of Chase making his way through the crowd, carrying two beers, she wondered if the little frisson of awareness that struck every time he came near was always going to be there.

Watch it, Gunny. Proceed with caution.

After he'd pulled them out from under the bull's raging hooves, there were no further incidents of the life-threatening variety, but there were plenty of fireworks that had nothing to do with the ones signaling the end of the rodeo events for the day.

Being highly attracted to the man one was contemplating getting to know a whole lot better was a good thing. Being bowled over by said man, to the exclusion of common sense, could not be allowed.

She had a mission in mind if Chase was interested. The look he was giving her said he was. This wasn't love, just two consenting adults coming together by mutual desire. She hoped.

This is crazy!

"Your beer." He placed a sweating glass in front of her.

"Thanks." Forget wild monkey sex. For the rest of her leave, it would just be nice to spend time with a man who wasn't her therapist and who didn't think she was crazy. "Would this be a good time to tell you you're fired?"

His grin was spontaneous and sinful. "You don't say."

Jane relaxed into her seat, grinning back at him. "I do say.

I'm feeling better. More in control."

She wasn't sure how to put it into appropriate words, but she felt lighter somehow. Freer. Not so caged in or crazed. "Thank you."

"Are you sure?"

"I'm sure."

"Then, you're welcome. You've made a lot of progress since coming here. You'll still have spots of trouble, but I'm okay with sending you back to light duty."

"That would be great."

He lowered his gaze to the glass he was twisting in slow circles. "So, you'll be leaving."

She should. There was nothing to be gained by flirting with danger. Except she had a ton of leave coming. And she should take advantage of the fact that Chase's ranch *was* the perfect spot to take a vacation.

There was also the kids' future to see about. She wanted to make sure he could pull off his promise to help them. "If you don't mind. I'd like to stay for a while longer."

"I don't mind." He looked up at her, his slow grin returning.

A minor earthquake rumbled in Jane's chest. This was not wise. The man was just too tempting for her military discipline to be of much use.

Ignoring the internal warning, she stood. "Do you want to dance?"

"Absolutely."

The band was good, but not as good as the moment he pulled her into his arms and, in a slow shuffle, skillfully guided her around the outskirts of the other dancers.

Tonight, she wasn't the soldier down on her luck who'd arrived at the ranch two weeks or more ago. She was a woman enjoying an evening with a wickedly handsome man.

Ripples of pleasure skipped up her spine. There was just one tiny little problem. If she wasn't careful, she could stay here, moving around the dance floor with him forever. But tonight, she didn't care.

She rubbed at the slight ache starting to bloom in her hip. Not an overt movement, but one that caught her dance partner's attention nonetheless.

"Your hip's bothering you."

In the last few days, there had been no pain, no limping, no need for her to massage the ache out. "Too much exercise, I guess."

"I have just the fix for that."

At his audacious grin, Jane thought, *I'll bet you do.*

~ * ~

Chase was pretty sure he wasn't choosing the best course of action, but holding Jane close while she swayed loosely to the music had him thinking of something a little more energetic than dancing.

Of course, ending up at a secluded hot springs wasn't what he'd planned when he'd taken her to the bar. When Gus and Maxine had offered to take the kids to the youth dance, then home, he'd thought a quiet drink would take her mind off the nearly tragic events earlier in the day. Then she'd fired him with that sassy smile, and all he could think about was that her barriers had been eliminated.

From the moment he'd first set eyes on her, all dangerous-looking, furious at being forced to deal with what had happened, thinking she could take a swing at the world and forget the consequences, he'd wondered who the woman was beneath the tough Marine exterior.

TWELVE

He'd seen how being with Zach and Abby softened her in ways she probably wasn't even aware of. And he'd been slowly seduced by how she'd taken them under her wing, even though she didn't want to. The way she'd become their champion when she was determined to be anything but was the hardest to resist.

He parked by the hot springs he'd discovered on the BLM land bordering his ranch. Without taking his eyes off her, he reached into the back seat and grabbed the blanket he kept there. "Nature's hot tub. A long soak will do wonders for your hip."

Her elegant brows shot up. "If you say so."

Her sky-blue eyes flashed another message entirely. His heart rate zoomed, flying high like a home run, hit out of the ballpark.

When he climbed out of the rig, she was right behind him. A full moon softly lit the night, bathing her in a soft glow. He hesitated, wary of the reckless feelings that had driven him to bring her here.

It wasn't that he couldn't be tempted to do more than soak the lady's sore hip. It was simply that he hadn't engaged in recreational sex since he was a teenager. And, he had an uncomfortable feeling that one fleeting roll in the hay with Jane, or in this case, a splash in the hot springs, wasn't going to be enough.

She studied him for a long moment as if to gauge his intentions. He didn't know what they were either, but making up her mind, she turned her back on him and began to strip off her shirt.

His response was automatic and instantaneous. In three long strides, he closed the distance between them, helping her pull the tank over her head. Taking his breath away, she faced him, wearing a thin wisp of a lacy bra.

Curling her fighter's hands in his T-shirt, with a sigh of pure womanly appreciation that knotted his gut with stirred-up passion, she returned the favor.

When a Marine took on an assignment, she followed it through to the end. Suddenly, more than life itself, Jane wanted this man's lips on her and then some.

She laughed at herself. Some things in life were just too delicious to ignore. This moment with Chase Russell was one of them. She was done being the good girl. If life could wink out in the space of one heartbeat, then before it was her turn to go, she was going to break her own rules and be bad. Very bad. She would worry about the fallout later.

Quickly unlacing her boots, she sat to pull them off, and stripped down to her underclothes before sliding into the steaming water. Welcoming the mini-wave that lapped her skin when Chase joined her, she sank up to her neck, leaned against smooth rock, and closed her eyes for one blissful minute as the heated water gurgled along aching muscles.

A large, bare foot slowly slid up her leg. Her eyes flew open. She fell straight into a smoldering look that spoke directly to the heart of the ravenous hunger growing inside her belly.

"Nice skivvies."

Tilting her head, she grinned. So, she liked sexy, silky underwear when she wasn't on duty. "Great hideaway you've got here."

"I've always earned high marks for finding creative solutions to problems."

Jane believed him. "Is there a girlfriend somewhere out there we should talk about?" She waved a distracted hand in the general direction of *out there.* Since she was about to do her best to ravish him, it would be a shame if she couldn't.

"Not anymore."

"What happened?"

"She broke it off after Nate's attempted suicide."

"I'm sorry." What woman in love would kick her man when he was down?

The narrowing of his eyes signaled he wanted to be done with talking, which was okay with her, except it was his turn. "Any chance of a reconciliation?"

"No. It was my fault. I wasn't so easy to get along with right after."

Taking hold of her ankles, he gave a tug that had Jane gliding through the water and settling provocatively on his lap. In the name of that living she'd decided earlier was top priority, she caught his shoulders for balance, anticipation digging her nails into hard muscles.

Strong hands skimmed her face, then advanced to the pulse point at the sensitive place where her jaw met her neck. She stretched to give him better access, which he took full advantage of with plundering lips.

Craving the feel of him, she was glad of the quick movements that had her bra and panties gone, tossed haphazardly beyond the edge of the steaming water. He cupped her bottom, bringing her closer to his unmistakable erection. Her breath caught as her most intimate place slid along the hard length of him.

"Chase?"

He settled her snugly on his lap, his grin reaching out to her from those sinfully sexy, cinnamon eyes. "Jane?"

When he flattened a hand between her breasts, testing

the swell on each side, coherent conversation became nearly impossible. She gave it a shot anyway. "I should warn you. I take prisoners."

"So do I. Now, shush."

"Yes, Sir." When his lips took hers, she was ready.

Rational thought was long gone by the time he broke the kiss off to reach for the pants he'd discarded. "I have protection."

"Let me." She took the packet from him. Despite the heat of the water, a shiver worked its way over her skin. "I want you. Now."

"Not yet." With both hands around her waist, Chase lifted her until he could leisurely love each breast in turn, his tongue making magic, taking her close to the edge, but not quite setting off the fireworks she was craving.

Denying her what she wanted—Chase buried as deeply as possible inside her—skillful fingers dove into her center. Jane gasped at the pleasure ricocheting to short-circuit what was left of any intelligent thinking.

"My. Turn," she rasped, initiating her own plundering. She wanted to make him groan, pay him back for making her lose her mind.

Reaching between them, she found the length of him and applied her brand of magic until his eyes blazed, and his breath came in quick puffs. When they were both close to the flash point, she sheathed him, then, tantalizingly slow at first, slid him into her warmth until he was buried as deep as she could take him.

He groaned.

Her eyes fluttered closed as she began a slow pump that escalated with need and purpose, until delicious, mind-blowing spasms stole her breath and shot them both out into the cosmos.

Oh. My. God! It was the last sane thought she had.

As she floated the last mile to earth, Chase rested his forehead against hers. His voice rasped, his breath not quite even, "Okay. Now that you've taken me prisoner, what are you planning to do with me?"

Her muscles robbed of all strength, she leaned against his chest until his thick words penetrated the fog of scattered reality enveloping her. For the first time since she'd let him drive her to this place, she began to wonder what in the Sam Hill she was doing.

They were supposed to be passing ships in the night. Anything more lasting couldn't...wouldn't work. She took a deep breath, then forced herself to leave the comfort of his lap.

"What's wrong?"

She hadn't meant for tonight to feel like something that could last longer than the rest of the leave she had left. "I—"

"Jane?" Her name came out in an understandably confused growl. She was just as completely thrown by the feelings rolling roughshod through her.

Like an unlucky lightning strike, it hit her. Instead of taking a prisoner, the Marine had been captured. Wasn't that a hilarious joke?

Chase reached out to her.

She pushed away. "I'm sorry. It's not your fault. I thought I could do this." She waved a hand that included them and the indulging hot springs, hiding her ballooning fear behind a shallow chuckle. "But I gave up one-night stands a long time ago. What the hell do you say after?"

"I want more than one night from you."

The words shocked Jane. She couldn't lie to him, so she opted for a cold splash of truth. "Don't make this into something it's not. In less than two weeks I'm heading back to my unit."

"They're your family."

She swallowed, then nodded.

A muscle jerked in his jaw. He stared at her with those flashing eyes that said more than she wanted to hear. Then, his expression cleared, which was scarier still.

He shrugged. "Don't worry about it. I get it."

Did he? She'd just had the most incredible, wild sex with the guy, but becoming attached was something she couldn't risk.

"What are your plans for Zach and Abby?"

He climbed out of the hot springs. Moonlight glinted off his wet, naked body, quickly stirring her up again. When he straightened, he cast her a look that no longer invited her into his world. "Get legal custodial guardianship. See if I can adopt them. That hasn't changed."

Her heart hurt as she slowly followed him out of the pool. "That won't be easy."

He pulled on his jeans. His eyes flashed. "That's not your problem."

Jane grabbed her clothes. He knew where to stab to do the most damage, but he was right. It was no concern of hers. Hadn't she told herself that all along?

She dressed quickly, keeping her eyes averted from the ripple of hard muscles as he dragged on his shirt. Sucking in a painful breath, she did her best to ignore how incredible being with him had been.

Refusing to let him see, she crossed swiftly to his truck, climbed stiffly inside, and waited until he joined her. In reality, the drive back to the ranch took a mere fifteen minutes. In the charged silence, it felt like forever.

THIRTEEN

C hase didn't shout or swear. He didn't kick anything. He wanted to, but he didn't.

Instead, he wiped the sweat from his face with his shirt sleeve, staring at the neatly stacked wood he'd just chopped for the fireplace. It wasn't enough to keep his mind off the woman who was turning his world upside down. And, not in a good way, if you asked him.

He headed for the barn and the bales of hay that needed to be restacked.

Sleep was non-existent since all he could think about was the satiny feel of Jane's skin, the vanilla scent that was all hers, and the way she tasted like cotton candy and an out-of-control roller coaster ride, mixed.

He climbed the ladder into the hay loft to begin moving the haphazardly piled bales closer to the trap door in the floor that was just big enough to allow one to be dropped through to the main floor.

Getting Jane out of his system, if that had been the idea behind their *encounter* last night, wasn't going to be possible. A brief, casual affair was no longer the answer. The discovery had kept him rooted to the spot when she'd gone into full retreat.

He heaved the bale he was carrying. It was his fault, the predicament he was in. She'd always been totally up front about her intention to get well enough so she could return to her real life.

He was the one who'd let things get out of hand. But when she'd slipped off her shirt, his good sense had taken a hike, and his brain had quit working.

Narrowing his eyes, he suddenly stopped, the next bale he'd grabbed straining his muscles. Could he talk her into staying? Not for the kids, but for him? Did he want to?

He snorted. It was a long shot. And, since he'd never considered himself stupid enough to buck the odds, why was he trying to work out how to convince the woman she should change her whole life for him?

She wasn't a brand-new, shiny Mustang he could take home from the showroom. She was a living, breathing, sexy... Marine. And therein lay his problem. She had a right to the life she loved so much.

He put the bale on the stack he was building. With an uncomfortable sense that some things were just inevitable, he closed his eyes and rubbed the bridge of his nose.

For the first time in his life, he wanted to fight for someone. And that someone was a brooding, controlled, edgy Marine.

He needed to have his head examined. Still, there was no denying it. He was taken with the lady. It'd ambushed him. The staggering feelings were not what he was searching for.

THIRTEEN

She was dangerously appealing in every way possible. Too intelligent for her own good. A fighter for what she believed to be the right thing. And she had a heart so gentle and loving hidden beneath her soldier's stoic exterior.

He'd probably been lost from the first moment out by the punching bag, temper running hot, chin jutted out, eyes fired up with determination. He should be ecstatic that he'd found a woman who could complete the rest of his life. He wasn't. His lady love was planning to get on the fastest train out of Dodge.

"Mr. Gus says the mommy cat and her babies are in the hay loft, and I'm not to go up there by myself." Abby's announcement broke into Chase's disconcerting revelation. "Will you go up there with me?"

"Sure thing." *Jane.*

The barn was the size of a small house, the hay loft spanning the whole length. The sound of kittens mewing came from the farthest corner.

Anticipation tugging sharply at his gut, Chase reached down to pull the little girl the rest of the way up the ladder into the loft, pointing her in the right direction. "Over there in the corner."

~ * ~

At the sound of Chase's spine-tingling baritone telling Abby where to look for the barn cat's babies, Jane nearly missed the next rung on the ladder. Blindly, she grabbed his hand. It wasn't until his fingers closed around hers and a fiery reminder of the night before raced up her arm that she asked herself what she thought she was doing.

With the hope she could escape the shocking way her body lobbied for a repeat of their sexy interlude at the hot springs,

145

she'd come out to the barn looking to work on the motorcycle. On the way, she'd gotten waylaid by Abby.

And here she was, breasts-to-manly-chest with the guy she was trying to get out of her system. Unfortunately for her, the look in his heated eyes made no secret of his desire for a repeat performance. God help her. She wanted it too.

Fighting for breath and the space to get her mind working again, she pushed him away.

"Miss Jane. Look!"

Jane forced her wobbly legs to take her to Abby, where she squatted next to the child. Hypersensitive to Chase's movements, she knew the minute he made himself comfortable on the far side of the little girl.

She frowned. Didn't he have anything better to do than to keep her senses misfiring in random abandonment?

"Aren't they beautiful?" Abby breathed reverently. "Can I touch one?"

"Sure." Chase gently placed a marmalade kitten in Abby's outstretched hands.

"Oh." The word was drawn out in breathless delight.

He passed one over before picking up the remaining furry ball, cuddling it close to his chest. Before he could see how moved she was by the picture they made, man, woman, and child mooning over the little animals, Jane buried her face in the dark gray tabby fur.

Don't be stupid! The Corps needs you. This is not your home. Not your man, either. And this sweet little girl isn't your daughter. Don't pretend otherwise.

"Can they come live with us in the house?"

Chase shook his head. "They have to stay with their mommy for a while longer."

"What if their mommy goes off and leaves them?"

Jane sucked in a breath. Innocent children shouldn't have to worry about their mothers leaving them.

Chase brought his little kitten up to his face until he was nose to nose with the little fella. Her heart lurched. Suddenly, she was as eager for his answer as Abby.

"Well, the mommy is a barn cat, so she won't leave them until she teaches them how to hunt and take care of themselves."

"But, if she did, could we bring them into the house and adopt them?"

He put his kitten next to the anxious mother cat, took Abby's and lined it up with its sibling. His gaze met Jane's over the child's head. "Yes, I guess we could."

Her fragile control splintered. How in the hell was she ever going to leave if every time she turned around, she was tempted to join this pseudo-family he was making?

She handed over her kitten, taking care not to brush her fingertips along Chase's hands, opting for another distraction instead. "Who wants to go to town and get an ice cream cone?"

"Me. I do." Abby jumped up, her cast conking Jane on the knee. The sharp rap wasn't nearly as painful as knowing that soon she'd be leaving this astonishingly irresistible man behind.

A grin spread across his handsome face. "I know just the place."

Argh! Not again!

Not long later, at Sam's Scoops, an old-fashioned ice cream parlor on the main drag running through Lone Pine, Jane and Abby sat on one side of the booth, and Chase and Zach on the other, licking away at the tallest vanilla cones she'd ever seen.

The quaint shop smelled of homemade waffle cones, root

beer, and sugary sweet ice cream. The black and white checkerboard floor was pleasantly offset by a brightly colored mural on one wall—families enjoying ice cream treats, the men in top hats, the women in long, spring dresses, sitting around ornate tables in a bustling courtyard filled with blooming flowers.

In deference to the hot day, on the way into town, Chase had stopped at the local department store to buy flip-flops for the kids.

When was the last time she'd worn flip-flops? Jane couldn't remember, and so when she'd come across a pair with bright red sequins, she couldn't resist. Even the man now running a bare foot over her ankle, sending enticing shivers up her leg, had picked out a pair to replace the worn boots he'd been wearing that morning.

She rolled her eyes, scooted her foot under her seat where she hoped he couldn't reach. Slowly, she licked her ice cream, ignoring the flicker in Chase's eyes.

She wasn't falling for the guy. There was no question in her mind. No matter how tempted she was to stay, when it came time for her to go, she was headed back to Parris Island.

It could be the man was doing her a favor, showing her that life didn't have to be all spit and polished. Maybe it was time to do some things she hadn't done in a long time, or even ever.

Just because she had her duty didn't mean she couldn't occasionally take off her uniform and have a bit of fun. Not that being a Marine wasn't fun.

She looked up from her cone just as his clever foot found her pant leg. His gaze fixed on her mouth, arousal simmered in clear brown eyes.

Jane blushed, her imagination taking off more than her

uniform for him. To break free of the breathless tension simmering in the air-conditioned air between them, she glanced out the window. Across the street was a bookstore. The Book Nook. It gave her an idea.

Finishing her cone in a hurry, she scooted out of the booth. "I'll be right back."

Chase raised an inquiring dark brow. She gave him a cocky grin for an answer.

Later that night, after dinner was finished and the dishes were done, Jane settled on the couch with her purchase. A small fire flickered in the fireplace.

Gus had gone out on a mysterious date for the evening. Chase, Zach, and Abby were playing Monopoly. The mouthwatering smell of freshly popped buttered popcorn filled the room.

"Miss Jane. Look. I'm the dog."

Jane couldn't help it. She'd never been this close to feeling like she was part of a real family. "Lucky you."

"Do you want to play?" Chase's deep voice was inviting.

She held up her book. "No thanks, I think I'll read."

Abby came to stand by the couch, leaning against Jane's legs. "What are you reading?"

The wistfulness in the little girl's eyes pulled at her heartstrings. *Harry Potter and the Sorcerer's Stone.*

She'd heard of the Harry Potter books, of course, but never made time to read any of them or even to see the movies. When she saw the first book in the bookstore, she decided it was about time she got on board the Hogwarts Express.

"It's your turn." Zach grouched at his sister.

Abby ignored him, looking up at Jane with bright, expectant eyes. "Will you read to me?"

"Sure, but don't you want to finish your game first?"

"No." She handed the playing piece over to Chase, then crawled up beside Jane on the couch. "I want you to read to me."

"Okay." Surprisingly, she was a little nervous about reading out loud into the suddenly quiet room with only the crackling fire for backup.

Glancing first at Chase, who raised both brows, then rolled the dice; with a little flutter of excitement in her belly, she opened the book and started to read, "Chapter One. *The Boy Who Lived.*"

~ * ~

Chase could see Zach would much rather be listening to the story about a boy wizard than playing a game with him, so he stretched his arms over his head and yawned. "If you don't mind, I'm too tired to finish playing. You guys wore me out today."

Zach's chin jerked up. "Are you sure?"

Chuckling, he began gathering up the game pieces. "Yes. Go listen to the story. I'll put all this away."

Glancing over at him, Jane's smile took Chase on a roller coaster ride. Despite all that had happened, he was still glad she'd fired him.

He put the game away, then divided the popcorn into smaller bowls, one for each of the kids, one for Jane, and what was left for himself. He stoked the fire, then stretched out on the floor near her feet. Propping his head on one hand, he let himself be drawn into a story about a boy who'd lost his parents and never fit into the inflexible family in whose custody he'd been left.

Jane gave each character a different voice, drawing him in

further. Her British accent had him drooling.

Abby crawled into her lap. Zach leaned against her shoulder. There she was, his warrior woman, telling a tale of survival to two kids trying to get along in a ruthlessly unpredictable world.

That was the moment Chase truly realized this was his family—Jane and two kids, all three engrossed in a story that mirrored their own lives. Except for the magic, of course, but maybe they could find some of that, too. They were going to need magic to make it so they remained together.

So taken by the sound of her voice, she was in the middle of the second chapter before he realized Abby had fallen asleep, and Zach was valiantly losing his fight to stay awake.

Wrapping his hand around her slim ankle to snag her attention, he tilted his head toward her two dozing listeners. Reluctantly, he stood, lifting Abby into his arms. "I'll put them to bed."

He nudged Zach's foot. "Come on, buddy. Time for bed."

Zach yawned. "I'm not tired."

Chase shared a grin with Jane. "Time to go to bed, anyway."

His eyelids at half-mast, Zach didn't argue further but followed Chase up the stairs, flopping onto his bed without changing into pajamas.

The small room had two twin beds. Smiling at the absolute rightness of putting the kids to bed, he settled Abby on the other twin, removed her shoes, and tucked them both in.

Stopping at the door, he looked back at the slumbering kids. Who would have believed when Jane first came to him that one day, shortly, he would be Jonesing for the four of them to be one big happy family?

Down there in the living room with Jane reading to them,

passion ringing in her sweet voice, he'd wanted the woman more than ever. If he didn't find a way to convince her to stay, his life was going to be emptier than when he'd walked away after failing his brother.

Except for the kids. He'd still have Zach and Abby, and he was more determined than ever to give them the loving home they deserved.

When he went downstairs, he found Jane in the kitchen, cleaning up the remains of their popcorn. "They're sound asleep."

She looked over her shoulder at him, her eyes moody, kissable lips pressed mutinously together. Tension snapped around her slender frame.

He loved the look of her, the feel of what was suddenly crackling between them, and decided it was about time to prod her just a little. See if he could edge her closer to finding a good reason to stay.

"That was a fine performance you gave tonight."

She gracefully lifted one shoulder and let it fall. Turning back to the sink, she sank her hands in the soapy dish water and pulled the plug. "It's a very clever story."

He stepped up behind her, close enough she couldn't spin around. Plucking a dishtowel off the counter, he wrapped his arms around her, captured one of her hands, and thoroughly wiped it dry.

He spoke next to her ear, his breath brushing the ends of her short, spiky hair. "My favorite part was when the glass enclosure vanished and Dudley fell into the snake pen."

Jane went perfectly still. "He deserved it."

When she started to scoot away, he grabbed her other hand, drying it with equal attention. "My second favorite part was your British accent."

She turned her head, her smiling lips coming within cen-timeters of his. Her breath was sweet, like the peppermint she liked in her coffee. Stormy eyes locked on his mouth. Her voice was a husky whisper. "I was stationed in England for a while."

He tossed the towel back on the counter, then turned her into his arms. The sound of the house settling for the night surrounded them. The smell of melted butter lingered.

A need for more than basic, scratch-the-itch sex slapped at his nerves. The hell with it. Tugging her against his chest, he fused their lips with a punishing hunger that she quickly took over.

Efficient, long-fingered hands grabbed his shirt front, rip-ping it open, popping buttons across the floor and counter. Those hands found and tested the strength of his chest, eagerly making their way south. When they got to his navel, he sucked in a hard breath, pounding desire making him rock hard.

He grabbed her exploiting hands. "Wait a minute."

"I believe you started this, Doc," she said, breathless.

"And I want to be with you at the finish line, Marine."

Her lips quirked, her watchful eyes focused, very cool. "Are you sure you have the stamina?"

That did it. Chase lifted her onto the breakfast bar. His hands burrowed under her shirt, pushing the cotton up until he could flick open the front latch of her bra. He palmed each heavy globe in turn, rubbing his thumbs over pebbled peaks.

When he replaced his hands with mouth and tongue, great shuddering breaths racked her. She arched into him, her fingers furrowing through his hair, dragging him closer still. Her skin was soft as silk, her scent hot, destroying whatever strategy he'd started with.

Who was giving whom a reason to stay? Chase could no longer think straight. She had him panting. Tugging the shirt over her head and tossing it to the side, he brought his hands to her face, holding her there while practically drowning in the aroused depths of her eyes.

He pulled her to him, nipped her bottom lip, and took advantage when they parted. Tongues danced together. His breath caught in his chest. Greedy hands skimmed over her shoulders, down her arched back to take handfuls of her luscious bottom. He scooted her until her heat was right up against his.

"I want you in my bed."

She huffed out a breath, her beautiful blues clouded over with unmistakable arousal, her lips quivering with it. "I won't lie to you or make promises I don't know how to keep. I can't stay."

"I know." Then he lied to her. "It doesn't matter."

She looked at him for a long minute. He saw the moment she surrendered. "I need you. Deep inside me. I want you. There. Now."

That, at least, was something they agreed on, Chase thought hazily as he lifted the woman into his arms. Carrying her up the stairs and into his bedroom, he kicked the door closed behind them.

FOURTEEN

W hen he woke up, Jane was gone. The first sign of sunrise filtered through his bedroom window, which faced the back of the house. It was open, and he could hear the thud of gloved fists pounding furiously on the punching bag.

They'd slept little during the night, spending most of the dark, intimate hours exploring, discovering. The headstrong woman would make a rock break a sweat. He wasn't near that tough, but he'd given as much as he'd taken.

Listening to her attack the poor punching bag, he grinned. If the Marine was a little unnerved this morning, she could join his club.

He dressed, checked on the children, and then went down to make coffee. He watched through the screen as Jane, giving the punching bag a break, did a warmup that rivaled the toughest military physical training.

He should feel bad about lying to her last night. He had no

excuse except that he wasn't ready to let her go. If he'd told her how deep his feelings ran, it would have scared the soup out of her.

The ache in his chest scared him, too. He'd just had a few more days to get used to the idea of loving the woman, even though she was planning to pack her sea bag and then head out of his life for good.

No limp in sight, she took off at a slow jog. At a loss for any ideas on how to convince her to stay, Chase took the easy way out—for the moment, anyway—and retreated to his office.

A few hours later, when the phone interrupted his paper-work, he was grateful. With his mind running in circles, he hadn't gotten much done after she'd returned and gone straight to the shower. All he could think about was joining her.

Tossing his pen down, he grabbed the insistent device. "Hello?"

"Hi, Chase. It's Beth."

"Hi, yourself. You're at it early." He leaned back in his chair.

"I'm calling about your kids. I have news."

"Why doesn't that sound good?"

"Their mother filed a missing children's report on them."

"Zack and Abby Malone?"

"Yes. I searched my database and ran across their pictures."

"Are you sure? They told me their mother died in a motor vehicle accident."

"I'm positive. I can fax over what I've found."

"I'd appreciate it."

Chase snapped the phone back onto its receiver. Waiting impatiently for the information to come and unable to sit still, he paced to the window to stare at the mountains glowing in the early morning sun.

Distracted by his longing to talk Jane into staying, anger fought with deep disappointment and won. He couldn't blame the kids for lying, but he intended to find out why.

The fax machine activated. Ten minutes later, his temper marginally controlled, the faxed papers gripped tightly in one hand, he found them in the kitchen.

They were all there. Jane, freshly showered, hair brushed off her forehead and drying in appealing wisps, poured orange juice. She placed the glasses on the table in front of the kids. Gus was at the stove, cooking French toast. Zach and Abby slouched at the table, obviously just out of bed.

His heart hurting, Chase stared at the group that had no chance of becoming a family now. Mentally, he kicked himself. He shouldn't have fallen so deeply in love with the idea. Jane was leaving, and no matter what their home life was like or why they'd run away, no parent who posted missing children reports would sign papers that gave custody of those kids to a virtual stranger.

"I just got a call from my friend at Children's Services." Four pairs of eyes swiveled in Chase's direction.

"It seems your mother, Goldie Malone, has filed missing person reports on both of her children, Zach and Abby. Do you want to explain what's going on?" Doing his level best to stay calm, he pinned Zach with a stern look.

The teenager jumped up from the table, eyes blazing, fists punched down at his sides. "Okay, so she's not dead. She may as well be. She doesn't want us, and you can't make us go back to her."

Not sure he believed the boy, Chase didn't try to stop him when he fled the room. Instead, he turned to Abby, hoping she could shed some light on this comedy of errors. Though her eyes were round and frightened, her baby face held too much weariness and way too much knowledge of the way life shouldn't be.

"She gave Zach a hundred dollars and left us at a homeless shelter. She wants to marry George. George doesn't want kids." As if that explained it all, and perhaps it did, she quietly followed her brother upstairs.

When he looked at Jane and saw the defeated resignation on her beautiful face, his frustration broke free. Not against himself. Or the kids who'd lied to protect themselves. Or the woman who held his heart in her hands but couldn't believe she had a right to happiness. All his anger targeted the irresponsible woman who'd treated her children's hearts and safety so cruelly.

This time, he wasn't going to walk away. From the kids. Or from Jane.

~ * ~

Their mother wasn't dead.

Jane swallowed the raw emotion that rose like bile into her throat. She'd almost fallen for it. This picture Chase had started to make her believe in. A family of her own that no one could take away from her.

She sank into the chair Zach had deserted. "What are you going to do?"

"I'm going to have a little talk with them." Chase shot her a hard look before heading for the stairs.

Gus placed a plate of French toast in front of her, shaking his head. "Poor kids."

His sympathy galvanized Jane. She caught up with Chase before he reached the upper landing.

"What will talking accomplish? Shouldn't we just hunt the

158

mother down and…I don't know…make her pay somehow?"

He stopped mid-step. Giving her a chance to back down, he gripped her shoulders, pulled her close, and ambushed her with a quick kiss. "Nice idea, but the system doesn't work that way."

She bristled, feeling the heat of dashed hopes along with reawakened awareness on her skin. "I know, but I don't see what talking is going to accomplish."

A grin spread across his face. If it were an option, Jane would have fallen for him right then, maybe even used the L word.

"You're a remarkable woman, Jane Donovan," he told her before firmly settling her against his chest, his heart thumping beneath her hands.

The kiss was the kind of kiss every schoolgirl dreams of; the kind that leads to happy-ever-afters. The only problem was that Jane didn't believe in storybook endings.

A little dazed, when he released her, she followed him into the kids' room, where a belligerent teenager swung to face them. "We're not going back to her."

Chase didn't give Zach any wiggle room. "I don't want to send you back, but I have to know the whole truth before I can make any claims."

Her stomach fluttered. The man was pretty remarkable himself.

"You said we could stay," Abby whispered brokenly, sitting forlornly on her bed.

The man staking his claim on Jane's heart sat beside the little girl. Lifting her onto his lap, he turned his razor-sharp gaze on Zach. "So what's the deal with your Mom?"

The teenager glared down at his shoes. "She keeps chasing after these rich dudes. They say they'll marry her, so she dumps us in a shelter somewhere and takes off with them. But they don't, so then she comes back and takes us away again."

Squaring his shoulders, Zach's eyes overflowed with the hurt and pain of being rejected over and over. Jane remembered how that felt. Anger boiled in her chest on the kids' behalf. Mothers like that shouldn't be allowed–

Zach kicked at the rug, covering a small square of the floor. "She doesn't want us. She only wants the money the state gives her for keeping us. That's why I thought, if we could live with Pop—"

"Can't we just stay here with you and Miss Jane and Gus?" Abby begged, tears slipping down her cheeks as she clung to the man gently cradling her.

The little girl's misery sneaked into Jane's heart, squeezing hard.

Marines do not cry! Impotent fury threatened to spill from her lips in the form of colorful sailor words that shouldn't be uttered in front of innocent children.

Abby switched tactics. Her sweet eyes pleading, she gave Jane a wobbly smile. "You and Mr. Chase could get married. Then it would be all right if you adopted us. If you pay her money, Goldie would never take us away again."

As though he thought the idea a perfect answer to their problem, Zach looked first at her, then at Chase, hope springing into eyes that perfectly matched his sister's.

Shocked at how reasonable it sounded and how truly appealing the thought of marrying Chase Russell was, Jane didn't dare look at the man.

"That's not going to work." The words flew out of her mouth in a hurry, jagged as if she'd just chewed on slivers of glass. "I mean, I'm not going to be here much longer. I have to get back to the base."

A wife and mother? That took courage. And maternal skills. All she knew how to be was a soldier, and most recently, not a good one at that.

As the hope in Zach and Abby's eyes faded. Jane straightened. She had to make them understand. "Chase and I can't get married."

"Why not?" Zach demanded, his fists perched on his hips.

"We're not in love." She looked at Chase. His handsome face was impassive, though his eyes burned darkly with an emotion she was afraid to put a name to. "Right?"

Those shards of glass got sharper. "No, I suppose not."

He supposed not?

For a second, Jane thought she saw disappointment skip across his face and was surprised by the wallop it gave her. But then it was gone, and she figured it must have been a mistake.

Understandably desperate, Zach wouldn't give up. "That doesn't matter, does it? Do you have to be in love to get married? You like each other. Isn't that enough?"

She suddenly wanted it to be, but knew it wasn't. She respected Chase, admired his dedication. Sex with him was a whole lot more than she'd expected. Heartfelt. Fantastic. Fourth of July fireworks.

When everything was said and done, they could end up friends. But, married?

Chase couldn't take his eyes off Jane and the internal battle he could see she was fighting. His stomach clenched.

He loved the lady; had plotted to find a way to get her to stay. But marriage? Now that the kids brought it up–

He knew what it took to make a marriage work. Plain stubbornness and a love that could survive anything. His parents had set a good example.

The Marine had enough stubbornness for both of them, but from the look on her face, she didn't feel the kind of love it would take. And why should she? He needed time to convince her.

"I'm not looking for a quick fix here. If things are as bad as you say with your mother, I need a plan that will convince the authorities that you should stay with me permanently."

Zach looked skeptical.

"Promise you won't do anything rash. Give me a chance to work things out." He spoke to the boy but looked straight at Jane.

Zach hesitated before agreeing, "Okay."

Suddenly, four people in the small room were one too many for Chase. Moving Abby to the bed, he rose, coming face to face with Jane.

Her barricades were up, as though the night they'd spent together never happened. Of course, marrying him, even to give Zach and Abby the break they needed, was the last thing she'd bargained for when she'd come to the ranch.

He shouldn't give it a moment's consideration either, but then, why did he feel like he'd just been soundly kicked in the gut?

~ * ~

It took only moments for Jane to make her way out of the house and to the barn. The good thing about her good buddy, Mr. Harley, was that the bike didn't make her heart ache with dreams that couldn't possibly come true.

She clamped on a helmet. Pushing the big machine out of the barn, she climbed aboard, revved up the engine, and let the resulting roar block out the heart-stirring image of Chase

Russell sitting on a child's bed, offering comfort to a little girl who had no one else to turn to.

Flying out of the ranch yard, she turned toward town. When she passed the graveled road that ended at the hot springs, she made a sharp U-turn, gunned the engine in a roar that brought the front tire off the ground.

In that brief second before regret flitted across his handsome face, Chase had reached out to her, silently asking her to join him in his crusade to take care of Zach and Abby. A crusade she'd pushed him into taking on in the first place.

But he was asking too much.

Parking the bike, she left the helmet on the seat and walked up to the steaming water. The scent of sulfur filled the thick air.

Squatting at the edge of the natural spa, she rested one arm on her knee. The other skimmed the swirling surface, her mind filling with images of what she'd done the last time she was there.

She snorted, cursing the blush that warmed her skin. A marriage for convenience was absolutely out of the question. Only a kid who found himself in a hopeless situation would think of that solution.

Chase understood it wouldn't work, right? It was her bad luck that the man had grit, exuded it with a sexy, come-hither aura that drew her like a she-wolf to her mate. Whether he was helping Gus repair a fence, teaching Zach and Abby to ride horses, or talking a Marine off the ledge she'd backed herself onto—for those things alone, she could fall hopelessly in love with him.

Which was why she wasn't going to go there. The military, with its inherent long separations, was not easy on a family, no matter how much love was involved. If she took the risk, then lost Chase—because no matter how hard you tried, holding on to the one you loved the most didn't work—it would kill her.

"It can't work," she told the gurgling water. "Thanks to Chase, I survived the last go-around. But, one more hit like that, with a man I could honestly give my whole heart to, I won't survive it."

The water had no answers. Jane hung her head in acceptance. Better to keep their relationship on a casual, friendly, sexual-ships-passing-in-the-night level.

She would go home, get back into the swing of things, and forget all about her little interlude with the most spectacular man she'd ever met.

Jane mounted the Harley. It was too bad because if anyone could make a believer out of her while at the same time cut through all that discouraging, social services red tape, it would be the man who was getting too close to her heart for comfort.

"Wouldn't I love to stick around and see him do it," she whispered to the bubbling pool.

~ * ~

Later that night, when the phone rang, Jane was sitting alone in the kitchen, having one last cup of coffee before she turned in. She'd spent most of the afternoon after returning from the springs implementing a workout regimen that would rival her early days in boot camp. When her leave was up, she was going to be physically, as well as mentally, ready to go back to work.

Gus had returned to his cottage after dinner to hunker down to a John Wayne movie, he said. She'd read a few more chapters of Harry Potter to Zach and Abby, but Chase was noticeably absent, closeted in his office, making calls.

None of their hearts had been in the story. She'd finished up by making sure the children got to bed without any mishaps.

Swallowing the last of her coffee, she drummed her fingers on the table. She trusted Chase to do what was right for the kids.

When the phone rang again, unable to sit still any longer, she decided to check on his progress, telling herself it was all about Zach and Abby and not about wanting to see if she could coax one of his crooked grins out of hiding.

The office door was opened a crack, his back to her as he stared out the window, the phone scrunched between his ear and shoulder. She leaned against the door frame. From her vantage point, she had a great view of the man, which she took advantage of. There was a good portion of the night left.

"There's got to be a way."

Dragging her gaze away from his perfect backside, she studied her cleanly trimmed fingernails.

"They said Goldie abandoned them." Frustration rolled off his shoulders like a thick fog coming off a South Carolina bayou.

"They don't want to go back to her."

His back stiffened. Annoyance became anger. "I get it. She's their mother, and she has rights. But, don't the kids have rights too?"

Pulling roughly on a piece of loose skin on one finger, Jane started to steam, too.

"I know the courts rarely find in favor of children in these cases."

Her heart got heavy. What had she expected? One of those miracles? Zach and Abby didn't stand a snowball's chance.

A sniffle had her spinning around to find both kids right behind her. By the scared looks on their faces, she knew they'd been there long enough to overhear.

She glanced over her shoulder. Chase was still busy with his call. The siblings weren't stupid. They'd had the score battered into them long ago.

She urged them toward the living room. "I thought you guys were in bed."

"We couldn't sleep." Zach's defiance was gone. All that was left was a frightened kid who didn't know what to do next or whom to trust.

"Chase is doing the best he can."

"Goldie's not going to let us stay. Neither will a judge." He faced her, his arm snaking around his sister's slumped shoulders. "He's going to send us back. It's not fair."

No, it wasn't. "You don't know that."

"I wish we could stay with you and Mr. Russell." Abby's brown eyes were awash in unshed tears. If wishes were currency— "You'd make the best mom."

Uneasy at the little girl's assessment, Jane gulped back tears. "Maybe things aren't as bad as they sounded."

She didn't know what else to say; how to make what was most likely going to happen easier for Sergeant Malone's kids.

She knelt, pulled them both tightly against her chest. When they clung to her, she cleared her throat and whispered roughly. "You'd better go to bed now."

Shoulders sagging in resignation, Abby clung to Zach. They trudged up the stairs. Jane's heart was broken.

When she'd first come to the ranch, she'd thought nothing could be more horrible than waking up in a Madrid hospital and being told by a harried doctor that Linus was dead. And then, realizing it was her fault because she'd failed to do everything she could to keep him safe.

She was wrong. Watching Zach and Abby drag themselves up the stairs was far worse.

FIFTEEN

"I'm not letting Zach and Abby go back to that woman." Chase balled his fist. The hills on this side of the ranch were dark shadows beyond the illumination from the yard light. "There has to be a way to get a judge to see how dangerous it is to give them back to her."

On the other side of the line, Beth heaved a sigh. "Unlikely, but worth a try. What do Zach and Abby want to do?"

Chase had no intention of telling his friend what Abby's wish list included. "Do you know a judge who would be sympathetic to their case? I want custodial guardianship."

"Let me work on it."

After Beth hung up, he returned to his desk, swiping from his mind the murmur of Jane's voice as she'd read to the kids earlier that night. He'd wanted to join them, sit at her feet, and give in to the illusion that whatever was happening between the two of them was something special.

He thumped his fist on the desk. It *was* something special.

At least to him, it was.

He massaged the back of his neck. It'd been hard not to go to her, but he couldn't forget the look on her face when the kids asked why they didn't get married.

The sight of her recklessly pushing the Harley to its top speed to get as far away from the debacle in the house as she could stayed with him. He wished he could call her a coward for that. Instead, all he wanted was to snatch her up and tell her everything was going to be okay.

But how could he make that promise? Maybe marriage right this minute wasn't the right answer, but it hadn't taken him two shakes of a lamb's tail to realize that was what he wanted. Spending the rest of his life waking up to Jane would be pure heaven. Giving her family, growing old with her, icing on the cake.

He'd let ego get in the way, hadn't offered one convincing reason why they should give it a try. And, before he could make it right, explain they were more than two people offering comfort to one another at a time when they both needed the warmth of someone who understood and cared, she'd taken off.

There had to be a way to keep the Marine in the game long enough to get her to switch teams. Satisfied that he had a direction to go in, nebulous though it was, he went to work on the kids with renewed purpose.

Half an hour later, Gus interrupted. "I'm heading over to Maxi's. She needs some help birthing one of her horses."

From the day he'd hired Gus to help with the restoration of the ranch, Chase had found a good friend in the older gentleman. Before he could rein in his curiosity, his mouth got away from him. "You're sweet on the lady, aren't you?"

His foreman turned a ruddy red but stepped further into the room. "Same as you're sweet on Miss Jane."

Sweet on Miss Jane? Wasn't that the truth? Heaven help him.

Chase smiled ruefully. "Jane's not interested. Seems to me Maxine is, though."

"Maybe. Maxi was my wife's best friend. Donna's been gone six years now. It's been lonely for both of us since she passed on."

He didn't know what made him ask, except all of a sudden, he wanted to know how an older man with more experience went about courting a woman. "Are you going to ask her out for dinner?"

Gus snorted. "Have you asked Miss Jane out?"

Not if you didn't count their drink in the bar after the rodeo, but it was a little late for conventional dating. They'd gone from, *May I have this dance*, straight to sending rockets to the moon. "No."

"That's probably a good thing. She'd likely turn down an ugly fella like you, anyway." Humor sparked the old gent's eyes before they went as serious as a papa wolf protecting his pup. "That gal's been hurt real bad. She needs gentle handling and a lot of understanding…I'm thinking about asking her to marry me."

He almost swallowed his tongue. "Jane?"

"Maxi."

Chase released his breath. Gus and Maxine Connor. He hadn't seen that one coming. "Good luck to you." And he meant it.

"Maybe you're of a mind to settle down too. A young man like yourself should have a wife and family." With a wink, Gus sauntered out, and not long after, his handyman's old pickup rattled by on the way to Maxine's.

Thinking about Gus's less-than-subtle hint, he closed down his computer, turned out the lights, and went upstairs to his room.

Maybe a good night's sleep would clear his thinking. But when he climbed into bed, he missed having Jane next to him. Holding her. Getting familiar with the softness of her skin. Discovering what intimacies made the blue of her eyes burn hot like the flame of an acetylene torch.

Frustrated on more than one level, he groaned, flipped off the too-warm covers, flopped onto his back, and started counting sheep.

Exhausted from a restless night, the next morning, he went to check on the kids. Zach and Abby were gone. Their meager clothes, everything. It was like they'd never occupied the spare room.

~ * ~

"There's no sign of them." Jane met Chase by his truck, drank in the pacing, worried man, praying the churning in her stomach would subside.

She should have known this was going to happen. Should have anticipated Zach and Abby's desperation last night.

They were gone. She wasn't going to be able to keep bad things from happening to them.

When she'd told Chase about the kids overhearing his telephone conversation, he'd sworn with a viciousness that warmed her heart. She was heading to search the barn next.

But first, unable to stop herself, she leaned into him, stepping closer still when his hands grabbed her around the waist. "We'll find them."

"Of course we will," he agreed gruffly as though he found it harder than she did to accept help. "Why in Sam Hill did they run? I told them I would work on a way to keep them."

Jane stared into his troubled eyes, swallowing hard. "It had nothing to do with you. Trust is hard for people like Zach…and me."

"You're something special, you know that?"

He lowered his head until his lips brushed hers, but it wasn't enough. Despite her earlier decision to keep things casual between them, Jane turned the press of their lips into something more demanding. Framing his face with her hands, she proceeded to kiss his socks off.

Quick enough, reason surfaced. She cleared the voracious need from her throat. "With Abby still in a cast, they can't have gotten too far on foot."

To keep from grabbing the delicious man again, she stuffed her hands in her jean pockets and stepped back. Her only excuse for this unmitigated hunger was that she'd missed being in his bed last night.

"I'd better contact search and rescue; let Beth know they're on the move."

"I'll take the bike out and check the roads."

He cupped her cheek with one hand. "Thanks. I know how difficult this is for you."

She swallowed hard at the gentle understanding in his touch. Turning quickly on her heels, she went into the barn. Anxious to get on the bike and ride, she pulled the Harley off its kickstand, pushing it toward the front of the building and freedom.

She was as bad as the kids. She knew exactly what they were feeling. The urge to start the engine, hop on, and keep riding until she met the setting sun was overwhelming. A rustle up in the hayloft caught her scattered attention. Voices raised in angry whispers floated down to her.

She parked the bike, berating herself for being so taken up with her anxiety, she hadn't checked up there. "Zach? Abby?"

Footsteps shuffled up the ladder. Zach's head and shoulders appeared in the opening. When he saw her, he came down, jumping from the last step.

"Where's Abby?"

The boy kicked at the straw. "Up there. She won't come down."

Grabbing his shoulder, she checked him out head to toe. Thank God he was okay. She snagged his gaze. "You took all your things with you. Were you leaving?"

He nodded. "Before she went chasing after George, Goldie threatened to take Abby away and not tell me where she was. It's my job to take care of my sister. I promised Pop I would. I can't let Goldie have her again."

She briefly closed her eyes. She'd thought she had it bad growing up without a family. How would it feel to be yanked from your sibling? It would feel like *she'd* felt when she lost Linus.

She drew in a deep breath. "You didn't go far."

"Abby wanted to say goodbye to the kittens. And then... I didn't know where to go."

"All right. Go tell Mr. Russell. He's worried sick."

Zach's chin dropped to his chest. "He'll want to get rid of us, won't he?"

"No, Zach. He won't. He's in the house calling his friends to help look for you and Abby."

After the teen left the barn, she climbed into the hayloft. Unable to see Abby at first, she could hear the kittens and followed the soft mewing. The little girl was tucked behind a bale, holding one of the little marmalade cats snugly under her chin.

"Abby?" She sat on the floor next to the little girl, shaking off the horror of almost losing her. "What are you doing up here?"

"I don't want to go back to Goldie. She's not nice to Zach." With a choked cry, Abby threw herself and the kitten into Jane's arms.

Swallowing a lump of relief, she smoothed the child's fine hair. "It'll be alright."

"I'm scared."

"Me, too. You scared the crap out of us, leaving like that. How was I, or Mr. Chase, to know something bad didn't happen to you and Zach?"

Round, sorrowful eyes flooded over. Abby smeared the trail of tears running down her cheeks with the back of her fist. "But you're a Marine, like my pop. You can't be scared."

She shook her head at the child's reasoning. There was a time she'd thought the same thing. "Soldiers are afraid sometimes, too."

Behind her came the soft scraping sound of Chase and Zach climbing into the loft. They sat next to her on the straw-covered floor. Chase picked up two of the kittens and gave one to Zach.

"Why?"

"Well, it's hard to explain, but even though we try very, very hard to be good, there are times when it's not enough, and we make a mistake."

She looked over Abby's head at Chase. What she saw shining in his cinnamon eyes ruffled her edges. Still, she met the look head-on. She'd been sent to the ranch to make sense of her troubled past. She wasn't going to be afraid any longer.

She tightened her arms around the child in her lap. "I made a mistake, but I understand now, and it's time to move on."

"I don't want you to go."

"I have to, baby."

"You're going to protect us from the bad men. That's what my pop told Zach and me." Abby sniffled, entirely too grown up for her tender age.

If she let herself, Jane could drown in the darkening eyes devouring her. "That's exactly right."

"Can I write to you sometimes?"

Resting her chin on the top of Abby's head, she finally broke free of Chase's consuming gaze. "Yes, and I'll write back."

"Promise?"

"I promise."

The familiar feeling of being buried alive hovered at the edge of her vision. She was back in Madrid, losing the life she'd known. To wipe away the image, she concentrated on how right it felt to be holding Abby. How her engines turned over when the Doc gave her *that* look, like he was now. The sharp, clean smell of stacked hay anchored her, along with the soft purring that came from the kitten Abby held.

Pushing the cloying feeling away, she took a steadying breath. Abby cuddled closer. Beside her, Zach shifted restlessly, burying his face in his kitten's fur.

Jane didn't hide from the memory that had her in its crushing, debilitating grip when she'd first arrived on Chase's doorstep, so desperate for his help. She let herself see things as they were, finally accepting she couldn't have done anything different.

Maybe she hadn't been discerning enough, was a little

too trusting, too—not blind—but involved in trying to give Linus a better life. With a little girl and a baby kitten settled comfortably on her lap, Jane suddenly realized she liked that about herself and wouldn't change that part of her personality after all.

Profound relief washed over her. She'd won the battle.

The only regret she had was leaving behind this man in whose care she would place the children. It made her heart ache, but she couldn't risk the loving, stable life he would give them by taking him into the soldier's life she was heading back to.

~ * ~

As their gazes melded, Chase witnessed the moment his long-legged, tough Marine emerged from the dust and smoke of her internal battle. Her victory swelled in his chest. A triumphant grin spread across her beautiful face. In the next instant, he recognized the decision that sprang into her baby blues.

They would see about that. No way in hell was he going to make it easy for her to walk away, but this was her moment, and he couldn't be prouder.

Right then, he knew nothing in his life was ever going to be the same. He'd been hit hard; fallen completely in love with an honor-bound, courageous woman who'd fought with her internal demon and won.

Gunnery Sergeant Jane Donovan was no longer the wounded Marine his Uncle had deposited into his care. She was magnificent. For the first time in his life, he wanted to take a woman— this woman—into his heart and keep her there forever.

The next day, he swiveled in his chair, staring out his office window. It was time to take his own advice and stop hiding out.

With Zach and Abby to consider, he decided, no matter what happened between him and Jane, he would stay on the ranch. Life here was—he laughed—okay, not simpler, but certainly more rewarding.

If Jane could defeat her failures, he could do something about his own. With the power of that thought urging him on, he made several calls. One to his brother. Others to his agent and publisher. Last, he left a message for Beth.

He watched his lady go toward the barn, the children following happily behind her. She'd announced at breakfast, they were going to wash the Harley, and Zach and Abby's glum expressions had perked up.

She was different today. The anger she'd brought with her when she'd first arrived was gone. The Marine didn't need him anymore. The irony of that had him shifting restlessly in his chair. Now, he was the one who needed her.

Last night, long after her nightly reading, she'd come to his room, and they'd made slow, lazy love as two lovers did, who for that moment in time, wanted to be nowhere else.

He'd felt the strength of her desire in the slender arms that held him. Heard the quick catch in her breath as he'd deliberately touched her. And watched, breathless, as she'd come apart in his arms.

They hadn't talked about her leaving. He wasn't quite ready for that, and anyway, it would come soon enough.

He rubbed the back of his neck. He wasn't cut out to be a Marine groupie. He wanted more from her, but first, he had to fight for Zach and Abby. She would understand and respect that.

The phone rang. Pivoting his chair around, he checked the caller ID before picking up on the second ring. "What did you find out?"

"Goldie Malone's not going to relinquish Zach and Abby. She wants them back. Pronto," Beth said.

"I want to fight for them."

"You're only going to get one shot at this, Chase. If Zach and Abby are willing to testify, and we can prove Goldie abandoned them, there's a slim chance the judge will consider their wishes." He heard the rustle of papers. "There are no other relatives. That will work in your favor; at least give you legal custody until the dust settles."

"So what's the next step?"

"I'll put a file together on Goldie. And one on you. I know a judge in Bend who'll take the case ASAP."

Chase wasn't surprised by the hard edge in his friend's voice. Or by how quickly she could make it all happen. Beth must have decided Zach and Abby were telling the truth. If there was one thing she couldn't abide, it was parents who didn't take proper care of their children.

When he hung up the phone, his mission shifted. It didn't take long to find Jane in the barn, alone, hunkered down, tinkering with the motorcycle. In her usual intense way, she used the wrench as expertly as she did everything else. At some point, she'd left a streak of grease across one cheek. It made her look more beautiful, capturing him as nothing else could.

"Where's Zach and Abby?"

She wiped her hands on a rag she grabbed off the seat of the bike and stood. "Gus took them to see Maxine's new foal."

"I just got off the phone with Beth."

"And?"

"Their mother wants them back. We have to go to court."

The vanilla scent she favored mixed with engine oil would always remind Chase of the stunning woman. "Beth wants Zach and Abby to tell the judge their side of the story."

Jane scowled at him. "And, try to have her declared unfit?"

"Beth says this isn't the first time she's abandoned them. She called in a favor. We have an appointment to see the judge on Monday to sue for custodial guardianship."

"It's hard to prove a mother unfit." Jane's voice lost all emotion.

"I know. But we have to try, don't we?" In this one thing, he was positive they agreed. They had to do what was necessary to keep the kids safe.

He was relieved when she nodded. This was his last chance to show the Marine what she was leaving behind. If she insisted on going, letting her go would be one of the hardest things he'd ever done.

"I need your help."

He grabbed her up, one arm around her shoulders, the other under her knees, eliciting a squawk that had a tremor of need rushing through him.

Her smug grin almost sent him over the edge. "What do you have in mind, Doctor Russell?"

He grinned wickedly back, his mind conjuring all kinds of explicit adventures. Long strides carried them across the ranch yard, into the house, and up to his bedroom.

Jane was pulling off her top before her feet hit the floor. Chase quickly got to work on her bra. "You're beautiful, you know that?"

He was rewarded with an embarrassed blush. He enjoyed keeping the woman off-balance.

"You're just after one thing." Her voice was a sexy rasp.

He laughed. It wasn't the thing she thought it was. "You can bet on it. How long do you think Zach and Abby will be gone?"

"Sounded like Maxine was planning to give them lunch."

"I want you," he growled.

"Not as much as I want you," she countered, her eyes going dark with a passion he planned to get on board with. "Now!"

"Yes, ma'am." He gave her a smirking salute, then tumbled her onto the bed.

Later...

"Guess what?" Abby was nearly bursting with excitement.

Chase glanced over at Jane, who hovered at the kitchen counter, wearing that devil-didn't-care expression he'd love to spend time wiping off her face. Her snug tee shirt was tucked into sinfully tight jeans, her sun-kissed hair finger-combed back into place as if he hadn't just spent an hour and considerable effort mussing the golden strands while he explored every inch of her.

He hadn't told her yet how he wanted her to help. That would have to come later, when they were alone again, and if he could keep his mind in the game, instead of letting the charge be led by his profound need of the woman.

He turned to the little girl tugging impatiently on his pant leg. "What, honey?"

"Now, Abigail," Maxine scolded.

"Maxi and I are getting married," Gus said, putting an arm around the older woman's shoulders. Maxine smiled shyly.

"They're getting married!" Abby shouted at the same time, a grin splitting her gamine face.

The room erupted. Abby clapped her hands in delight. Zach stood back, his attempt at looking uninterested a total flop. Even Jane lost her nonchalance, a smile lifting the corners of the lips that still bore the ravages of their recent lovemaking.

Tearing his gaze away, Chase clapped Gus on the back. "So you went and did it." He turned to Maxine. "Are you sure you want to get stuck with this old codger?"

Maxine's smile broadened, making Chase's heart ache. He wished he could make a certain Marine look that contented.

"I expect so."

Jane came to stand next to him. "Congratulations."

"Thanks." Maxine's misty gaze rested on Gus. "I don't know what Fergus sees in an old twig like me after being married to Donna, but the big dope says he loves me. I guess he must."

Was that what he needed to tell Jane? He'd do it in a heartbeat if he thought it would make a difference.

Maxine's brows drew together, her tone resuming the briskness Chase had come to expect from her as she glanced at Zach and Abby. "Can I have a word?"

Gus dropped a chaste kiss on Maxine's cheek. "Miss Jane and I will do something about dinner. Who wants to help make spaghetti?"

"I do! I do!" Abby tromped over to the counter.

Chase led the way to his office, not missing that Jane's eyes followed him. It gave him a small amount of satisfaction. Anticipation of the time when they would be alone again almost stole everything from his mind.

Closing the door behind Maxine, he offered her the chair across from his desk. "What's this about?"

"The children told me what you're trying to do. That's a noble thing you're doing, taking them away from that horrible woman and giving them a home here."

Maxine had warmed considerably since he'd had that first run-in with her at the hospital. "We're going to see the judge tomorrow."

"They deserve a decent place to live and people who love them. I want to help."

"I appreciate the gesture, but I'm not sure what you can do."

Maxine straightened. "I can speak to the judge on your behalf."

"I...um...would appreciate that." Stunned at the older woman's complete turnaround, Chase wished Jane's would be as easy.

SIXTEEN

J ane let Chase drag her by the hand into the Deschutes County Courthouse.

Last night, he'd asked her to come for Zach and Abby's sake so that they could present a united front. And, because he was holding her, their passion building, that knowing look in his eyes, understanding that she would still leave, she'd given in and agreed to do this one last thing for him.

Abby grabbed her other hand, eyes round with uncertainty.

She hoped everything would turn out all right, but wasn't completely sure she believed it herself. She sure as heck didn't want to be there when the kids were remanded back to their mother, but she'd made a promise, even if it was just in her heart. She wouldn't be that scared girl anymore. And she wouldn't abandon Chase when he needed her to stand at his side for the kids' sake.

Zach followed on their heels. Gus and Maxine were waiting in the immaculately clean lobby.

A neatly put-together woman met them halfway down the hall to the judge's hearing room. She must be Chase's friend at the county, Beth. "You're just in time. Our appointment with Judge Thomas is in ten minutes."

"Chase."

"Mom. Dad. What are you doing here?"

An older, feminine version of Chase and a middle-aged gentleman who had his son's wide smile rushed up to them.

"I called them," Jane told him. She'd found their number in the card file on his desk. "The more family support you can demonstrate, I thought the better chance you'll have a making your plea successful."

"You must be Jane." Chase's mother grabbed her hand, squeezed gently, lifted a cheek for her son's kiss, then turned to gaze at Zach and Abby with what Jane thought would be a grandmother's loving concern if she'd had any experience in that area. "Are these the children?"

Battered by an envy that took her back a lot of years, she decided then and there not to give it any credence. She was done letting the past rule her life.

"It's nice to meet you, Jane. I'm Mike. Thanks for calling us." Chase's dad held out a hand.

The Doc would look like his dad in thirty years, she decided. Straight. Handsome. Matured like fine whiskey. In charge of his world and at peace with it. His Mom's eyes were the same yummy brown, the woman's hair streaked daintily with white.

Jane fell in love with his parents on sight and was glad that when she left, he would have their help with the children.

"Hey, brother." A man slightly younger, thinner, and a bit taller than Chase joined them.

"Nate." Chase grabbed him, pounding his brother on the

back. "How…? You came."

"Mother."

Emotion pricked at Jane's eyes. This was how she'd always imagined a family would be.

Chase turned to her, his smile glorious. "Everyone, this is Gunnery Sergeant Jane Donovan. And these two rascals are Zach and Abby."

He'd finished introducing everyone when a uniformed woman stepped quietly into their midst. "Ms. Greeley, Judge Thomas will see you now."

They filed into the room where the judge waited for them, but Jane noticed Nate holding Chase back. Curious, she broke her own rule about not getting involved in other people's business and loitered. She'd never been good about keeping her nose out anyway.

"Listen, I want to make sure you know what happened to me, what I did, the hospital, none of that was your fault. I—" Nate shifted one shoulder. "—just lost it. You couldn't have stopped that."

"If I'd been there—"

Nate snorted. "You can't be with me twenty-four-seven, big brother."

Chase nodded. "How are you doing?"

Nate smiled wryly. "Better."

Jane believed him. Chase must have, too, because he gave his brother a strong-armed hug. Then, seeing her hovering, grabbed her around the shoulders and tugged her into the room and a seat next to him.

Judge Thomas closed the file he was studying, looked expectantly at Beth Greeley.

"Mr. Chase Russell is here to apply for custodial guardianship of Zachariah and Abigail Malone due to the deplorable circumstances in which the children were abandoned and left to take care of themselves by their mother, Goldie Malone. They've been living at Mr. Russell's ranch for the last three weeks."

The judge was a clean-shaven man on the sunset side of his sixties, Jane would guess. His gray hair was cut short, close to his head. The eyes behind round spectacles took in every detail of the people in his courtroom, reminding her of the Colonel when his stern gaze settled on Zach and Abby.

He'd probably seen a lot of child abuse in his career, but would he do what was right for the kids or go by the book?

In all the years she'd been a Marine, Jane had always gone by the book. It was just recently that she'd learned there were times when following your heart was the only option possible. She squeezed the strong hand that gripped hers, offering what silent support she could.

"Zachariah, Ms. Greeley has put together a very impressive file on you and your sister. As the Director of Crook County Child Welfare Services, I trust her judgment implicitly in these matters. But I want to hear from you. Why do you think the court should take you away from your mother and give responsibility for your well-being to virtual strangers? I understand Mr. Russell is not related to you in any way."

Jane's heart stopped cold. She was deathly afraid this man, who had the power of the law to change people's lives, wasn't going to do it for Zach and Abby.

Zach stood. A dignity older than his years lifted his young chin. "We don't have any relatives. Our father is dead. And Goldie doesn't give a darn about us. Every time she finds some new dude to marry, she dumps us in a homeless shelter.

186

This wasn't the first time, and if you don't let us stay with Mr. Russell, it won't be the last."

He put a protective arm around Abby, who'd stood with him. "I've been taking care of my sister since she was a baby. She deserves a nice home, with her own room, somewhere she can go to school regularly. She should have parents who care about what happens to her. Mr. Russell and Miss Jane love her. They'll take good care of her."

Her heart restarted with a resounding thump. Jane winced. He was right. She loved them both.

Judge Thomas pinned Zack with a measuring look. "What about you, son?"

"I'll be fourteen soon. I can take care of myself, get a job. It's Abby I'm worried about, Sir."

At that moment, the door to the courtroom burst open.

"Ma'am, you can't go in there." The guard who had brought them to the room tried to block the path of a blonde bombshell, unceremoniously pushing her way in.

"These children are mine. You're not going to take them from me," she said shrilly.

Beth stood and impassively introduced the newcomer. "Judge Thomas, this is Goldie Malone, Zack and Abby's mother. I informed her by letter of this meeting so she could present her side if she wished."

Jane scowled. Goldie Malone was beautiful, all decked out as though she'd just walked off the cover of some glossy magazine. Her hair was cut into a classic pageboy style, perfectly showcasing her memorable features. Makeup skillfully applied to attract attention.

Irritation disappeared from between dark, penciled brows as the siren flashed a hundred-watt smile calculated to bring the judge over to the dark side.

Who was the judge going to believe? This perfectly coiffed woman, or two troubled kids?

It was a good thing Chase had a strong hold on her hand because Jane would love to have a little one-on-one with the woman for the way she'd treated Zach and Abby.

Instead, she was thrown back to the one time she'd waited for news that her own adoption was finalized—she couldn't have been much older than Abby—only to find out she couldn't go with the Hollaways because her mother was still alive and wouldn't give up parental rights. It hadn't taken the nice couple long to find a kid they could take home. Soon after, they'd stopped visiting her.

She swore under her breath. Goldie knew how to play the system. It happened all the time. Zach and Abby were doomed.

Chase gently uncurled the fist she'd made in her lap. Taking both her hands, he laced his fingers with hers. When she looked up, he gave her one of those special smiles that promised to battle the bad guys and win.

She desperately wanted to believe he could. It'd been too many years since she'd allowed herself to depend on anyone but herself. Even with how he'd managed to bring her back from the brink of self-destruction and the times they'd spent entangled in his bed, she didn't know how to trust that he could keep that promise.

"Mrs. Malone, have a seat, please." Judge Thomas frowned, indicating an empty chair across the aisle from Jane, then addressed Chase. "Who are all these people?"

Never letting go of her hand, he stood and introduced everyone. When he was done, he pulled on her hand until she stood. "This is Gunnery Sergeant Jane Donovan."

The Judge's shrewd gaze shifted, resting on her for a long moment before he addressed Chase again. "In your file, it says you're a psychologist. You do work with war veterans?"

"Yes, Sir, I did. I have a ranch now, near Lone Pine. Zach and Abby are special to...us. We want to give them a stable home to grow up in."

Goldie sputtered angrily. Her polished veneer slipped slightly in the wake of the judge's sudden, hard stare. Small lines of self-indulgence appeared around her eyes. She didn't bother to readjust the short skirt that slid up to reveal the length of her thigh. "Hey, I have rights too, you know. You can't just take my kids from me without my consent."

"Mr. Russell has applied for legal custody of Zachariah and Abigail. If the documentation of abandonment in this file is accurate, it *is* within my jurisdiction to grant his petition."

For a second, hope fluttered in Jane's stomach. Chase might just pull this off.

Goldie tapped her toe against the linoleum in nervous agitation, then leaned back in her chair, her arms folding belligerently under her chest, lifting her cleavage. She shrugged one elegantly clad shoulder as if it was no big deal to run off and leave children to survive on their own.

The picture-perfect mother she'd worked hard to cultivate cracked. "I'm sure this is all just a misunderstanding. I would have taken them with me, but George—that's my ex-fiancé, George Keller—didn't want the brats... um, the children tagging along. I left Zach in charge."

The woman dared to glare at Zach. "He knows what to do when I'm gone. There was no reason to take off like that."

"So, you're saying you deliberately left these children, and not for the first time, it appears, at a homeless shelter? While you went off with Mr. George Keller to get married? Where is Mr. Keller now?"

The woman had the good sense to blush. The judge's deadly quiet tone rattled her tongue loose. "George can go to blazes. He dumped me in Vegas after I lost too much of his money."

"What is your source of income?" the Judge asked, seeming unmoved by her outburst.

Goldie abruptly stood, her hands coming to rest at her hips. "Don't you get it? Without the money their father left for their keep and what the state gives me for them, I have no income. There's no way I'll let you take them from me."

Abby jumped up on the other side of Chase. "Don't let her take us. She yells at Zach and hits him."

Embarrassment flushed across his cheekbones. Zach pulled on his sister's arm to get her to sit back down. "Abby, it's okay."

"But, Zach—"

"Sit down. Please."

Keep your cool, Jane. This time, it was Chase's calm voice she heard in her head, not her own.

"Mrs. Malone, you're mistaken about what I can and can't do. I've heard enough. If you'll please wait outside." Judge Thomas nodded to the guard who'd never left.

When he took Goldie's arm to escort her from the room, the woman jerked free, her pretty facade wrecked by outrage.

"How dare you! You can't get away with this." She spat the words at Chase and Jane.

Jane stood. Chase squeezed her hand, but she didn't need any help standing up to Goldie's wrath. She'd handled worse and survived just fine.

Wordlessly, she stared Goldie Malone down. No one, especially not this mean-spirited, self-indulged woman, was going to mess with Chase's family. Not if there was something she could do about it.

"Mrs. Malone, I will charge you with contempt of court if you don't go with the guard right now."

Goldie raised one hand, wanting to strike out. But then, with little grace, she spun and allowed the guard to escort her from the room.

"Gunnery Sergeant Jane Donovan. You're with the Marine Corps?"

Jane pulled her gaze from the closed door Goldie had gone through. Standing shoulder to shoulder with Chase, she faced the Judge. "Yes, Sir."

"Stationed at Parris Island?"

"Yes, Sir."

"I spent some time there. I don't imagine it's changed much."

"No, Sir." Jane allowed herself a brief smile. A silent understanding passed between them.

Semper fi.

"Are you planning to make your home on the ranch?"

Beside her, Chase went still. Jane felt Abby shift closer to him on his other side. Her small hand slipped into his. Zach stood tall beside his sister. Gus and Maxine hovered behind them. Chase's family was another row behind.

It seemed as though all eyes in the room turned to her.

How was she to answer? Her home wasn't the ranch. "I'll be returning to my base, but Mr. Russell will make a great custodial parent. I'll stay in touch." *If he'll let me.*

Her chest hurt with an unbridled hope that the judge would decide in Chase's favor. She held her breath.

"I see." He set aside their papers. "Well, Mr. Russell, you've stepped up to the plate for Zachariah and Abigail. I'm going to grant your petition for custody. A social worker will be assigned and will get in touch with you next week. In the meantime, Ms. Greeley will be your contact person. You can take the children home with you."

~ * ~

Chase blew out a breath of relief when Judge Thomas dismissed them, then told the guard to bring Goldie Malone back in. Jane looked stunned, as if she couldn't believe they'd won. He wasn't quite sure he believed it either, but he wasn't about to quibble over the victory.

Goldie shot daggers at them as they passed in the hall. Even the woman's venom couldn't diminish his elation. He had a chance to make a difference for Zach and Abby. He could give them a decent life. It was time for some whooping and hollering.

His dad beat him to it. A huge smile split his weathered face as he gave Chase a clap on the back. "How about we go out to dinner. I've just become a grandpa. That's worth a little celebrating."

Zach and Abby wore identical numb expressions, as if it hadn't truly sunk in that they had a whole new family who wanted them.

Abby was the first to crack. She laughed, jumped up and down, then grabbed the welcoming hand her new grandpa held out to her. "Hooray!"

"I can't believe we get to stay with you." Zach grinned, years of having to fend for himself and his sister falling away.

"I can believe it," Gus told the boy roughly, knuckle rubbing the top of Zach's head with undisguised affection. "That judge could see you was better off with Chase and Miss Jane."

Chase pulled Jane into a crushing hug. *See what we did,* he wanted to laugh with her. *We stood on the same battlefield and won!*

She blinked. He laid a big kiss on her parted lips. When he let her go, she was grinning, tears shimmering in her gorgeous blue eyes.

Clearing his throat, he grabbed Zach by the shoulder, "You did great in there, son."

Nate clamped them both on the back. "Welcome to the family, kid."

Amidst the group's excitement, it took a minute for the angry click of high heels to register. When it did, it was too late. Goldie snatched Abby as she rushed past.

Chase moved fast, but not fast enough to catch the woman as she sprinted toward the Courthouse lobby doors, dragging a screaming Abby with her.

"Put me down!"

"Stop that woman!" he shouted to the guards, who immediately drew their guns, scaring the crap out of him. "Don't shoot!"

Holding the weapons in plain sight, they pointed them up to the ceiling, positioning themselves between Goldie and the door.

Chase panicked. If anything happened to his little girl—

When she found her way blocked, Goldie spun around, dragging Abby with her. "You can't have the brat. I'm her mother. She's going with me."

Chase gathered himself to tackle Goldie, but Jane stepped between them. Never taking her eyes from the seething woman, she motioned sharply with one hand for him to stay put.

Against a driving need to get his new daughter back, Chase

hesitated. He either trusted Jane or didn't. Reluctantly, he followed her silent instructions.

"Let Abby go, Ms. Malone. You can't give her what she needs, and you know it."

"But she can give me what I need," Goldie jeered, yanking roughly on Abby's arm.

Chase swore.

Jane circled slowly. When all emotion faded into a deadly blank mask, he pitied anyone who had the misfortune to run into her in a dark alley.

She inched closer while continuing to talk softly. He went in the opposite direction, focusing all his energies on stopping Goldie. Nate worked his way around, too, until they outflanked her on three corners.

Goldie's eyes jerked from person to person, seeking a way out.

Please don't let Abby get hurt.

"Think about what you're doing to Abby, Ms. Malone."

Jane's attempt to appeal to the other woman's better nature was too reasonable for Chase's tastes. Goldie didn't have a better nature as far as he could see.

But he would agree to anything to get Abby back unharmed. "You can't walk out of here with Abby. The guards won't let you. If you just let her go, I won't press charges."

Goldie blinked, took a quick look at the guards. Finally realizing there was no way out, she released Abby's arm and crumbled to the floor.

Chase caught the child as she threw herself at him. Two of the guards holstered their guns, then took hold of Goldie, who was sobbing now, one on each side as they lifted the defeated woman to her feet.

"I didn't promise not to press charges. Book her for attempted kidnapping."

Chase had been so focused on getting Abby from Goldie, he hadn't heard Judge Thomas come up behind them. At the flare of temper in the older man's eyes, he made a mental note not to ever get on the judge's bad side, either.

Everyone gathered close, hugging first Abby, then Zach to make sure they were both okay. Jane hung back, her shoulders rigid. When their eyes collided, Chase dropped straight into the deepest corner of her soul. What he found there had him at last understanding why she was so determined not to let anyone in.

Buried deeper than he could have imagined was a profound fear of losing the person she allowed inside her defenses.

Her hands shook. He wanted to go to her, but that shimmer in her eyes ordered him to stay back.

How in the world could he convince her that two fighting the battle was far better than fighting alone? His shoulders dropped. She would never believe him.

Jane had her Marine buddies. It wasn't the same as having a loving family who would give up everything to be by your side, but he could see now, it was all she would allow.

He'd been told once by one of his patients that love didn't come easily to a soldier. For the first time, he could see why.

He didn't want to be the one causing this sweet woman pain. Because he loved her more than life itself, he would have to let her go.

That space in his chest where he'd made a place for the lady turned bleak and cold. At least he'd done the best he could by giving her the skills she would need to go back to the work she loved.

He told himself he was making the right decision, but in the end, all he could do was wonder how he was ever going to live without her.

SEVENTEEN

I t took Chase exactly one second to change his mind.

They belonged together. Jane might be giving up the fight before it was done, but he was not about to. As long as she remained on the ranch, he had a chance to convince her they were a team.

Everything from there happened so fast. They returned home after a lively evening at Pine Tavern, a family restaurant with a three-hundred-year-old pine tree growing in the middle of it. Letting the kids get to know their new family. His parents promise to spend some time with their new grandchildren.

And now Gus and Maxine's hastily thrown-together pre-wedding reception, which was doubling as Zach and Abby's introduction to the small community of Lone Pine, where they'd be growing up.

Through it all, no matter how hard he tried to draw Jane out of the shell she'd retreated into, she remained aloof.

She still read to Zach and Abby at night but avoided him like he'd come down with the plague. He was frustrated, but not from the lack of sex. The day of her departure was looming, and he still hadn't come up with a decent game plan that would guarantee she'd stay.

He couldn't keep his eyes off her as she mingled with the other guests.

"Want some punch?" Abby was dancing with excitement at the importance of the task Maxine had given her. She held out a paper cup.

"Thanks," He smiled at the little girl, nodding in Jane's direction. It was time to lure the mama tiger out of her den. "I need an extra one for Miss Jane, too."

Putting some of Zach's newly discovered swagger into his step so she wouldn't figure out he was on a mission to capture her, Chase carried the drink to Jane.

"What trouble are you girls getting into?"

"Beware Greeks bearing gifts, Jane." Beth flashed him a quick grin.

When Jane pasted on a false smile that had him grinding his molars, he took perverse pleasure in ambushing her with an unexpected kiss that he hoped had as much effect on her as it did on him.

She blinked, then turned a sexy shade of pink. "Beth was just saying she's shifted her caseload, so she can take on Zach and Abby herself. She's going to be their new caseworker."

She sounded a bit breathless. Excellent. So, she wasn't as unmoved as she would have him believe.

Later that night, after putting Abby to bed, he sat on the porch drinking a pop, planning his next ambush.

Crickets sang a serenade. The sky was clear and full of bright stars. The night smelled dry and sweetly of Juniper. A slip of a moon hung high above the horizon.

When Jane perched against the railing, crossing her arms over her chest, his gut tightened with the need to drag her onto his lap. But he could see in her stance, she wasn't going to give him a chance.

His time was up. She'd made up her mind to leave. Tomorrow.

"I have to go."

"No, you don't," he disagreed instantly.

"I can't."

"Yes, you can." He stood and took a different tack. "Zach and Abby need you." He swallowed hard. "I need you."

"Zach and Abby need *you*," she returned, confusion evident in the way she dropped her arms, waving a hand that encompassed the whole ranch. "Chase, I don't know how to be what you need or want me to be."

He swore. That's when it hit him. If he stood any chance at all of winning her over, he had to loosen the reins and hope to God, someday she'd come back.

He crowded her against the railing, cupped her beautiful face. Drinking in her beauty, both inside and out, he ran a gentle thumb along her parted lips. "You're the most gorgeous woman I've ever met."

Her blue eyes began to swim.

"The Corps is your family. I won't fight that, but I hope you know we're your family too."

He pulled her into the house, wanting to drag her up to his room to spend what little time was left memorizing every inch of her stunning body. Instead, he took her to the office, grabbed his phone, and dialed.

When his uncle's sleepy voice answered, he said abruptly,

"She's ready to come home."

Then he handed the phone to Jane, took one long, last look at the woman who'd moved lock, stock, and barrel into his heart, and without another word, dragged himself up to his lonely bed.

~ * ~

"I can send money to help out."

"No."

"I want to." Jane forced reason into her tone since Chase was not being reasonable at all.

She faced off with him just inside the kitchen. Her sea bag leaned against the wall. The heated brown eyes that had melted for her just days before were cool, staring at her with about as much emotion as the hard-baked clay out in his backyard.

He was closing her out. It was what she expected. What she wanted, right? It still hurt the same as being hit with mortar fire.

"Look, Jane, we'll be okay. You just take care of yourself."

"There's email."

"Sure." But they both knew the internet was a poor substitution for the real thing.

"I want to buy the Harley."

"No need, it's yours. A gift. I'll have it shipped to you."

His veneer cracked. Jane saw it coming. She welcomed the fierce kiss that rocked her soul down to her toes.

When it was over, he cupped her cheek with one hand and smiled sadly. "Travel safe, Gunny."

He hefted her sea bag, leaving her to say goodbye to the children. Shaken, she knelt to draw a quietly sniffling Abby against her pounding heart.

Closing her eyes, she memorized how the little girl smelled

of early morning breakfast, how soft Abby felt snuggled against her chest. She stowed the memory away along with that last kiss, where she could pull them out from time to time, when it didn't hurt like a tank crushing her heart.

"I don't want to say goodbye," Abby said fiercely, wiping away her tears with the back of one tiny hand.

"I won't say it either, then." Her eyes burning, Jane rose and reached for Zach.

Shaking her hand like a man, the teenager covered his emotions with a scowl. She pulled him in for a quick hug. "Take care of your little sister."

"You don't have to go."

"I have orders." *And maybe she believed that was why she was leaving.*

Crossing to the living room, she took one last look around. Signs of Chase and the children were everywhere. The coziness of their clutter would stay with her forever.

She had her duty. She was good at it. That had to be enough.

Jane forced her feet to move. Gus and Maxine waited near her Jeep.

The older woman wrapped her in a fierce hug, saying in a choked rasp. "I think you're making a big mistake."

Maxine quickly stepped back. "Come back for the wedding."

Fighting emotions that made no sense, Jane climbed into the rig. Buckling up so she couldn't change her mind, she firmly turned the key.

Sliding on her sunglasses, she took one last look at the people who'd given her sanctuary and brought her redemption.

Tears blurred her vision. She recognized the sound echoing off the hills surrounding the ranch for what it was. Her heart was splintering.

Silent tears fell down Abby's cheeks as she clung to Chase's hand. Zach kicked angrily at the ground with the toe of his sneaker. Gus and Maxine leaned into each other, their hands clasped as if they never intended to let go.

She didn't have any other choice. She *had* to go.

When she put the Jeep into gear, Abby's voice floated on the dry, hot air. "We should make her stay."

You can't because I'm a coward. Being a wife and instant mother... I don't know how to do that.

As she gunned the gas, she didn't hear Chase's response. How did you explain to a six-year-old how easy it was for an adult to make a total mess of her life?

They would all be better off without a dedicated soldier who was only just beginning to figure out how to go forward, instead of wallowing in the past like a cranky, battered cow trapped in a sucking mud hole.

Once she got gas and the last of Lone Pine faded from her rear view mirror, she decided to drive straight through. That way, it would only take three days of hard driving to get to the base, where she could put the pain of leaving where it belonged. In the past.

But the ache in her chest refused to be left behind. The more coffee she guzzled to stay awake, the more her mind insisted on going over the last month.

Even in the face of her uncooperative surliness, Chase had used every piece of ammunition in his arsenal to help her come to grips with Linus's death. And when Zach and Abby needed someone to be on their team, who had stepped on board without so much as a second's thought to how it would change his plans? Chase Russell was an extraordinary man.

She smiled at that, as the farther she traveled away from him, the heavier her heart got. Over and over, she told herself she wasn't *in love* with Chase. She was just grateful for what he'd done for her.

Liar!

And if by some strange quirk of fate she'd mistakenly fallen for the guy, it didn't matter. She'd get over it.

Liar, liar!

So the sex had been good—okay, spectacular. "I have a job to get back to," she said out loud for the hundredth time.

As she passed a sign that welcomed her to Colorado, Jane searched her heart and mind for the bitter Marine who'd been ordered to take her leave in Oregon. That Marine was gone, replaced by a woman who'd unexpectedly learned what it meant to live. All because of the persistence of a cinnamon-eyed man who didn't know how to give up and two audacious kids whose only wish was to be wanted by loving parents.

She looked back at how alone and isolated her old life had become, the same life she was hurrying back to. Her misery deepened. She couldn't help thinking that was what Chase had been trying to tell her all along.

She didn't have to be alone. She *wasn't* alone.

She banged the palm of her hand against the steering wheel.

Was it possible to grab the brass ring? Could she have everything she'd always secretly wanted? Just like Zach and Abby?

She was about to take an exit off Interstate 70 into St. Louis to get more gas when a utility truck ahead of her blew a tire, swerving uncontrolled from lane to lane before sliding to an abrupt stop against the guardrail.

Shaking with adrenaline pumped by the quick reflexes that had kept her from getting into a multi-car pileup in the middle of rush hour traffic, Jane stopped behind the truck. After a long moment spent catching her breath, she got out and leaned over the hood of her Jeep, counting backward from ten to calm her pounding heart.

When there was no flashback to another disastrous day, she grinned. Chase had given her back her life. The question was, what life did she want?

She gingerly approached the side of the truck to check on the driver. She found him, hands still gripping the steering wheel, slumped over, sucking in deep gulps of air, his forehead resting between his hands.

"You all right, mister?"

He turned his head to look at her, then leaned back against the seat. "Yeah."

"Do you need an ambulance?"

"No." His voice was firming up.

Jane backed up so he could get out, but just in case, she didn't go far. She stayed with the guy until the police arrived to offer assistance.

Shaken by the realization that life could be pretty darn short, that the even, measured life of a Marine base suddenly wasn't what she wanted, she got back on the road.

Then she laughed until tears ran down her face. She'd been spared again. Finally, she knew why.

When she unlocked the door and carried her sea bag into her house, her eyes burning and shoulders aching from lack of sleep, the place was like a sealed tomb. It didn't take her long to figure out why the silence left her feeling empty.

There was little of her in the sparsely organized rooms. No pictures. Just enough serviceable furniture to get by. No books. No children's laughter. No shoes left in the middle of the floor. No Chase Russell to sweep her into his arms and make passionate love to her.

The next day, when she reported in to the Colonel, she'd had time to wash the grime of travel off and get some sleep. Dressed in familiar fatigues, the comfortable rhythm of the base flowing around her, Jane gave the man who'd had a hand in saving her from herself a respectful salute.

"How are you feeling, Gunny?" The stern lines of Colonel Hawke's face relaxed into what the few who'd known the older Marine long enough would call a smile.

"Fine, Sir. I'm feeling fine." It was the truest statement she'd ever uttered.

"Good to hear it. I have your re-enlistment papers and a new assignment. A training position. It's yours if you want it." Speculation brightened Hawke's eyes.

He was offering her a great opportunity. One she'd waited a long time for. The problem was, she didn't want it anymore. And she thought he knew it, the old buzzard.

Her stomach took a tumble. Was she brave enough to turn down the perfect job on the remote chance that Chase might still want her?

~ * ~

Jane had been gone three weeks when Chase finally threw in the towel. At first, missing her so much, he couldn't think straight. He'd consoled himself with the reassurance that at least the kids were safe and happy.

He should be proud that he'd accomplished what he set out to do. And he was. The Marine had recovered from her wounds inside and out.

He'd been in touch with his brother. Nate was taking off on a road trip to clear his head.

Chase stopped outside the office. The door was half open. Zach stood at the window. Abby was perched on the edge of his desk chair, staring at the computer screen.

They checked every day for a message from Jane. And he read to them every night from the book she'd left behind, but it wasn't the same as having her here.

He kept thinking that he could get over the Marine, forget her, but it just wasn't happening. Though he was growing to love the children more and more every day, his food tasted like dirt, and the days were just too empty without the lady who made life sparkle with a magic he'd never known before.

"I miss her."

"We all do." Zach leaned over his sister's shoulder. "Is there an email from her?"

Chase moved back into the shadows of the hallway, unwilling to intrude on the kids and curious, too, if they'd heard anything.

Jane had let him know she'd gotten to Parris Island, and he should have responded, but he couldn't. Every tie, every connection, kept the memories of her too fresh.

He even avoided his uncle's calls. If he was going to move on with his life, he reasoned, he couldn't engage in long-distance, impersonal chitchat.

"Not yet," Abby echoed his thought.

"We have to come up with a way to bring her back." That was Zach. During the time Jane had been gone, he'd discovered the boy had remarkable skills in getting to the root of a problem.

"I could fall and hurt myself again." And Abby was the implementer. They'd gotten her cast removed last week. Chase shivered at the idea of her going through that again, even to bring Jane home.

"That's a good idea, but I don't think it will work."

"Why?"

"Well—"

"Oh, I know. We could kidnap Miss Jane, like Goldie tried to kidnap me. Except, she's very far away."

Chase swallowed the chuckle building in his chest. The kids might be going about it all wrong, but they had the right idea. It was time to bring the Marine home.

"Yeah, that probably won't work either, since I can't drive, and they'd put you in jail."

"Gus and Miss Maxine could drive."

"True. But maybe Miss Jane doesn't want to see Chase."

At night, Chase lay in the dark and wondered the same thing.

Abby squealed. "Zach, look."

"What?"

When Chase casually strolled into the office, he couldn't stop himself. Zach was writing on a scrap of paper. "Any new messages?"

The boy shoved the paper in his pocket. "Just spam."

Chase's curiosity, or maybe it was his urgent need to see Jane again, to hold her in his arms, took over.

She'd touched him—all of them—in ways she never intended. Suddenly, he knew what he had to do. He'd never rest easy until he had her in his life permanently. Even if that meant giving up everything and moving his new family back east.

The next morning, he explained his plan to Gus. Maxine, who'd gotten into the habit of coming over to cook breakfast *and* to go over the arrangements for their upcoming nuptials, poured pancake batter onto the sizzling griddle.

"Are you sure you don't mind keeping an eye on the place? It won't interfere with the wedding?"

"Heavens no." Maxine slid two steaming plates of pancakes and eggs onto the table. "We're not putting on a lavish show. Life's too short."

Chase had to agree with his smiling neighbor. Every minute that Jane was gone, every second he did nothing about the empty ache in his chest, was more time wasted.

He'd been a fool to let her go. At the time, he'd thought it was the right thing to do. You know, let the little dove fly free so she'd come back.

What hogwash. Who made up these stupid wives' tales anyway? He snapped his coffee cup back onto the table, got up, and took his unfinished plate to the sink.

"If we pack today, we can leave first thing in the morning."

"Maxi and I'll keep things going till you get back."

"I'm not sure how long we'll be gone. It could be a while."

"No matter." Maxine joined him at the sink. "You just go and bring that girl home."

Chase nodded. Intent on getting started as soon as possible, he missed the surprised look that passed between Zach and Abby, and that they ate in too much of a hurry, abruptly excusing themselves when they finished.

Later, as he threw what they needed into travel bags, all he could think of was how wonderful all their lives would be once he convinced Jane to let them stay.

Jane Donovan Russell would be a handful, their life together nothing less than explosive. Chase grinned in anticipation. He was ready to take her on. And if he had to use a little skin-to-skin therapy to bring her around to his way of thinking, by God, he would.

The next morning, he paced at the bottom of the stairs, glancing at his watch, wondering what could be taking the children so long. He'd roused them out of bed, fed them breakfast, and already loaded their bags in the truck.

Why was he still waiting for them to get dressed?

Anxious to be on his way, he stepped to the bottom of the stairs and shouted, impatience making him sound more frustrated than he intended. "Zach... Abby, come on. I want to get on the road before I go gray."

"We're coming." Abby jumped the last few steps down the stairs while Zach followed behind, moving slower than molasses as he yawned.

Chase couldn't believe it. Suspicion narrowed his gaze on the dynamic duo. "Are you planning to travel in your pajamas?"

Abby giggled as a vehicle crunched on gravel out front. Whoever it was leaned on the horn, a demand to come front and center that irritated Chase's already frayed nerves.

Spinning on his heel, he ground his molars. When he stepped off the porch, Jane was climbing out of her road-grimy Jeep. It was packed to the brim.

For a second, he took a step back in time. A black T-shirt stretched lovingly across her curves. It was tucked into the same black jeans she'd worn the first time he'd seen her and wondered who the heck the sexy lady was.

Boots encased her feet. The dark aviator sunglasses were in place, hiding spectacular blue eyes. A sassy grin split her beautiful face.

Chase's gut flipped as her long stride brought her to him. At the last minute, she hesitated, but then launched herself at him, her arms winding around his neck, long legs wrapping around his hips.

"What are you doing here? We were just leaving to come to you."

"You were?" Her grin softened. He could tell his announcement pleased her. Thank God.

If he had an ounce of self-preservation left, he would play it cool. But he didn't. Instead, he growled, pulling the word out into two syllables, "Yes!"

"I was miserable without you. It's all your fault for showing me what I could have if I just had the guts to reach out and grab it."

"Really?"

"Yes, really," she said with a grin.

"So, how long did it take you to figure it out?"

"You're going to make me beg, aren't you?"

For the first time in the weeks since she'd left, his world slid back into balance. "You bet your cute ass."

Jane laid a hungry kiss on his lips. He would have given in right then and there, but he wanted more from her. He wanted the same words he had planned to say to her.

He broke off the kiss. Leaned back enough to look into her gorgeous eyes. They sparkled with plain old-fashioned happiness and the sassiness he'd come to love about her.

"I was in St. Louis when I realized I'd left the best part of myself on a hilly ranch in Oregon. I love you, Chase Russell."

The admission came quickly, easing the ache in his heart. The morning sun beamed down its approval. Behind them, Abby clapped her hands, while Zach let loose an approving whoop.

"The Colonel once told me to take care of business, and then I'd be able to get on with my life. Well, I took care of business, and now I want to live my life...here...with you and our kids." Uncertainty suddenly filled her beautiful face. "If you'll have me."

"What about the Corps?"

She shrugged. "I was up for re-enlistment. I decided not to take the Colonel up on his offer. My life there didn't mean anything without you. So I emailed Zach and asked him if he would mind having a second mother."

The love that swam in Jane's eyes reached out to meet his. Chase didn't keep her waiting.

"I love you, Jane Donovan. You've taken my heart hostage. Will you marry me?"

"Yes, Sir!"

Jane demonstrated her willingness by planting her lips on his, kissing him until they were both breathless. Their audience finished cheering, then turned away in disgust.

"They need to get a room," Zach said to Abby as they left the room.

Chase heartily agreed. Jane was finally home in his arms, and he knew exactly how he was going to celebrate.

Thank You!

Thank you for reading Jane's Long March Home. If you enjoyed Jane and Chase's journey to home and family, it would make my day if you would write a review on your favorite reader sites and social media so others can find this book too.

If you're like me, you live a busy life and may have little time to follow authors whose stories speak to you. Want a Free story and updates on new releases? Sign up for alerts and my newsletter at https://www.susanlute.com/newsletter.

You can find me online at:
   Substack https://substack.com/@lutsusi3
   Instagram https://www.instagram.com/authorsusanlute/
   Facebook https://www.facebook.com/susanlute/
   Facebook Author Page http://www.facebook.com/pages/Susan-Lute/202040233153546
   BookBub https://www.bookbub.com/profile/susan-lute?

list=about

  Pinterest http://www.pinterest.com/sidella/

  And Goodreads https://www.goodreads.com/author/sho
w/1252907.Susan_Lute

Thank you for being a reader!

XO! Susan

Read on for a preview of... A Marine's Christmas Proposal

David Randall, once upon a time the top of his class at Stanford Business School, and more recently, Captain in the US Marine Corps, took a break from unpacking to watch his nephew run his toy truck around the boxes scattered through the living room.

"Brrrmm. Brrrmm."

Elijah turned his toy toward the open front door and ran as fast as his short little legs would go.

"Not so fast, buddy." David scooped him up just before the kid drove over the highly polished black pumps, stepping purposefully through the entry.

"More trouble than a platoon of Marines, isn't he?" Lilly Hunter's amused laughter followed right behind David's snort.

"It's a toss-up."

His aunt closed the door on the setting December sun before

214

planting a kiss on Elijah's temple. "But he's such an angel—aren't you young man?"

Setting her oversized black purse on the wood stove he hadn't had a chance to heat up to ward off winter's chill, she took in the chaos erupting from the boxes the movers had originally left neatly stacked against one wall.

Chaos reigned. For a Marine, even one who'd made the hard choice to become a civilian, it wasn't a good thing.

"Looks like you can use some help."

He frowned. In more ways than one.

He knew how to be a Marine, even one who was no longer on active duty. What he didn't know was how to be both mom and dad to a three-year-old.

His aunt was dressed in her usual business attire, a dark gray jacket over a pale pink blouse and gray wool skirt. As an administrative assistant to the owner and CEO of Banks Sportswear, she was from the old school and refused to relax her wardrobe to business casual. Graying hair hung in long curls to her shoulders, making her look more vibrant than your typical great-aunt.

"Michelle's coming over later."

A worry line etched between her perfectly formed brows. "She's working too hard. I was hoping to see her here this morning. I have something for her in the car."

Working too hard was his little sister—he would always think of her that way—doing her third year of general surgery residency at Oregon Health Sciences University.

"She's breaking away this afternoon to watch Elijah while I go to the interview."

Lilly ran a hand over the box on the coffee table marked Christmas decorations in his older sister Sarah's neat handwriting. Dark brown eyes welling with sorrow asked a silent question.

David shook his head, his heart crunching in pain. "Not this year. It was her favorite holiday. I can't."

Losing one of his soldiers had never been easy. Losing Sarah and Tom in a senseless traffic accident ripped his heart right out of his chest.

"Down!" Elijah demanded, kicking his feet, surprising David out of his misery by coming dangerously close to an important part of his anatomy.

On a choked laugh, he released the boy, almost dropping his nephew before the kid's lethal weapons got planted firmly on the floor.

Lilly chuckled.

He shrugged, fighting a smile. "He gets a little excited."

"So I see." His aunt knelt to Elijah's level. "Do I get a hug?"

Elijah threw himself into her arms as David's cell erupted with a country song. He plucked it off the box where he'd put it safely out of his rambunctious nephew's reach and watched from the kitchen while his aunt rained kisses all over the little boy's laughing face.

"Randall here."

"Captain. Wilson. I…um…how did the move go?" First Sergeant Brian Wilson, six months after retiring from managing troops, was now in charge of Human Resources for the Pacific Northwest Bank. The First Sergeant's promise of a sure job was one of the reasons David had left the Corps, packed everything he owned, and moved with Elijah to Portland. The other was to be close to the only family both of them had left.

The uneasy sound in Wilson's voice kick-started David's alarm. In all the time he'd known the retired Marine, the man had never been caught off guard. "Still unpacking. I'm all set for the interview this afternoon. My sister is going to watch Elijah."

"How's the kid handling…everything?"

A delaying tactic. This couldn't be good.

"He's doing okay." Except that an inexperienced uncle could never replace his parents.

"There's no easy way to say this, Captain. I just got word the bank is downsizing. They've put a freeze on hiring and canceled all interviews."

"Choo-choo!"

Wincing when Elijah plowed into his legs while pretending to be a runaway locomotive, all David could envision was his draining bank balance.

He ruffled the boy's blonde hair. "Any chance they'd make an exception?"

"I'm sorry, Captain. I tried. I know how hard it was to get here this fast."

A Marine never panicked. "Any scuttlebutt about openings at other companies?"

"None. The job market is tight."

Not a surprise. The feelers he'd put out hadn't brought any results until Wilson had called about the business analyst position.

"I can ask around. See what I dig up."

"Appreciate it." David disconnected and tossed the phone on the counter. His first assignment as Elijah's parent was to support the kid, and he was failing.

He straightened his spine. He could do this. Get a job. Keep it. Be a dad. Take care of Elijah like Sarah would want. She'd been the glue that had held the three siblings together when their family had broken apart. Now it was his turn.

He turned to Lilly as they had all those years ago. "Banks Sportswear doesn't happen to need a business analyst, do they?"

A Marine's Christmas Proposal, A Short Story
Amazon | BN | Apple Books | Kobo

Read on for a preview of... A Fool For Love

When the engine coughed, Alice York swore softly under her breath. Not at her beloved '55 Ford pickup—a classic she'd restored right down to the high-gloss, apple-green paint—but at the timing. The middle of rush hour traffic in Sellwood, a bohemian suburb of Portland, was not the place for the Ford's pampered engine to have a coughing fit.

"Just like a man," she muttered. "Flaking out right when a girl needs him the most. Hadn't expected that from the greatest cowboy in history."

Muscling the ton-and-a-half solid truck with its caravan-style canopy onto a tree-lined side street, Alice sighed in relief when they made it halfway down the block before Duke sputtered to a stop at the curb in front of an elegant, gray Victorian house. An elaborately carved sign read Martha's

Elder House.

She slumped in the seat and closed her eyes. She had to get to Dave's Classic Restorations, fifty-five miles away in Longview, where a job working on old classics like Duke waited. With exactly one hundred twenty-seven dollars and fifty-one cents in her purse, she had barely enough to rent a room and stave off hunger until her first paycheck.

Working on classic cars was good work when she could get it, putting enough money in her pocket so she could make it to her next destination, wherever that might be. And if she was lucky, along the stretch of road ahead of her, she could usually get in a painting or two.

But having to shell out a chunk of her scant reserves for new parts, plus take time to fix the Ford?

She banged her head gently on the steering wheel. She'd had one rule from the very first day she'd taken to the road. A litany of poor me was not allowed in Duke's cab. Melting into a puddle of panic was not an option.

Hood raised, her head, arms, and shoulders buried in the engine compartment, she tested connections. A door banged behind her with the force of furious anger.

A man's raised voice demanded, "Where are you going?"

Surprised, Alice jerked, hit her head on the hood, and saw stars. "Holy mother of–"

"You don't pay me enough to put up with that old man's insults!" A woman shouted, the voice shrill, pampered. Stilettos clattered past Alice.

Sneakers thumping the sidewalk followed, appearing briefly in her peripheral vision as she rubbed her scalp while blinking back waterworks.

Heavier boots stopped beside the truck. "You can't be serious,

Penelope. He's not saying you're a horrible cook. He just likes pushing your buttons."

All Alice could see were denim-clad legs, strong, masculine legs that would make any woman worth her salt salivate.

What now? Make her presence known? Or pretend she wasn't a witness to this very public domestic squabble.

Staccato beeps released a car lock again and again and again. Two car doors slammed, a high-octane engine roared to life, tires squealed, and the decision was taken out of her hands.

"Lady," the masculine voice, sharp with anger now, addressed her. "You can't park that monstrosity here."

Insulted beyond belief, Alice banged her head again and came out fighting. "The Duke is not a monstrosity!"

Dark brows knitted together, lips stretched in a straight line, the man belonging to the heart-thumping man-legs raised his snapping gaze from her backside to her face.

A flash fire of smothering heat burned from said bottom to her cheeks. *Holy mama!*

Her outrage drained while all her girly parts awoke with a shout. *Hello!*

His short, dark hair was painted by the sun with bold blonde streaks. Stormy blue eyes cut her no slack. The unshaven stubble covering a stubborn chin gave him a sexy look that would be hard for any woman to ignore. Alice was nothing but appreciative.

Faced with a long-neglected libido gone wild, she cocked one hip. Folding her arms across her chest, the temptation to trace the line of that stubborn jaw with fingers that itched to explore was hard to fight.

Glaring Sexy Guy probably wouldn't appreciate the grease she'd leave behind unless he liked his casual associations slick and dirty.

"You have to move it." His tone erased any humor her last thought inspired.

His glare didn't intimidate her. She'd seen worse. "Can't."

He matched her stance. "Why?"

"This truck's not going anywhere until I get a new fuel pump."

His glower deepened.

"Dad!" A young girl bounced down the front porch steps, interrupting whatever demand Sexy Guy was about to make. Blonde hair, trapped in ponytails, bounced. "Is Penelope gone?"

"Yes." He noticeably tugged on the reins of his temper for the sake of the child.

Alice gave him a point for good behavior.

"Did she take that creep Blake with her?"

His head snapped toward the girl. It was easy to follow his thoughts.

A sour taste sprang up in Alice's mouth. Had this Blake fellow been a creep to the blue-eyed child with the innocent face?

"Lucy, did Blake—"

The girl shuddered. "Ewe, Dad. No!"

Sexy Guy's shoulders relaxed. Mentally, Alice chalked a second point in his column.

He drew a deep breath. "Yes, they're both gone."

The girl pumped her fist, then turned to stare at Duke. "Wow. Cool color."

Her hand, lured by the enticing, shiny apple-green paint, stretched to stroke the truck.

Alice leaned forward to see if the kid had noticed the road

winding through the cityscape she'd painted last month on the length of that side of the truck.

She raised an eyebrow. Lucy cocked her head. "Is this truck yours?"

Sexy Guy placed a protective hand on his daughter's slight shoulder. "Luce, watch your manners."

The man making her heart beat like it was in the middle of an Olympic triathlon was a dad. Probably had a wife. That might have been the little woman who'd just made her temperamental exit.

As for his daughter, the girl was precocious and spoke her mind. Alice liked that in a person, whether a man or a child. But Lucy wasn't the only one who could be direct. "Yes, it is. And who might you be?"

"Lucy. I'm twelve." Sharp chin elevating, reminded Alice what it was like to be young and have to face unexpected, crushing changes. The kid tilted her head toward Sexy Guy. "That's Zach, my dad."

Doing her best to ignore frowning Sexy Dad, Alice stretched out a hand to Lucy. "Nice to meet you. I'm Alice York."

Very adult-like, Lucy met her halfway, pumped once, let go, and grinned.

Alice's chest swelled with the feeling of having hit a home run. Quickly, she stepped back. Making friends was okay. Getting attached to the girl's spunk wasn't.

An older man, with a striking resemblance to Zach, ambled down the porch steps to join them. He circled Duke with a low whistle before stopping next to Alice. "Is this your rig, young lady?"

She grinned. Young was a relative term. On some days like today, twenty-six didn't feel as young as it should. "Yes."

After introductions, he ogled Duke and the over-the-top gypsy-colored canopy nestled in the bed. When he was done, twinkling blue eyes fastened on Alice. "Beautiful. Just beautiful."

She swallowed sudden laughter. The older version of Zach had a lot more charm than his more youthful relative.

Lucy leaned into the old guy's arm. "Papa, Penelope, and Blake are gone."

"Good riddance is all I have to say."

Zach rolled his eyes. "Granddad, I'm trying to teach her manners."

"And a good father you are, too." Granddad slapped Zach on the back. "Those two were freeloaders. I'm not sorry to see them go."

"You're impossible. You know that, right?" The fight had gone out of Zach's tone, replaced by laughter threatening to pull his fascinating mouth into a crooked smile.

Sexy Guy clearly loved his grandfather. Grudgingly, she gave him another point. But just because he was racking up good-guy points didn't mean she could jump his bones the first chance she got, even though that was exactly the insane image floating through her surprisingly alert mind.

Stop staring, Alice ordered her out-of-control libido.

Sudden desire took a nosedive when he turned a stern eye in her direction. "You'll have to call a tow truck and get that—" eyes narrowed, he gestured rudely at Duke. "—moved as soon as possible. This is a no-parking zone."

Alice's hackles stood up to be counted. "We won't be here long if I can find a store that carries the part."

Zach's granddad rubbed his chin. "That truck's a classic. Won't be easy to find parts on a Friday night. And a holiday weekend to boot."

Frustration matching Zach Barret's replaced the temper she'd been holding with a tight rein. Broke down in a no-park zone in Sellwood, with no way to lay her hands on the part she needed, put a serious knot in the timeline she'd allotted to get to the new job. No job meant no money. No money meant being stuck. And unlike these nice strangers in their nice house, getting stuck in one place was the last thing she would let happen again.

Several calls later, she paced beside Duke, the cell still glued to her ear, while Lucy explored inside the caravan, and Zach and his grandfather debated the merits of Fords versus Chevys.

The bottom line was that the pump wouldn't be available until Tuesday morning, at which time her wallet would get considerably lighter.

When she was done ordering the part, Zach abandoned the debate with his grandfather. "If you release the brake, we can back this thing into the drive."

Thing? What the heck?

Sexy Guy didn't give her a chance to declare she didn't need his help, but opened the passenger-side door and waited for her to get in the driver's seat. When she didn't immediately take him up on his offer, the quick stare he shot in her direction suggested his already stretched-too-thin patience was on its last leg.

Snapping her mouth shut, she climbed in, pretending she didn't notice the flex of man muscles beneath the cotton shirt, sleeves rolled up to his elbows, as he put his shoulder to the jam and pushed.

"Granddad, give us a hand, would you? Miss York? Break?"

Swallowing the hitch of breathtaking up residence in her

throat, she released the break. John and Lucy pushed from the front. Zach put his impressive muscles to work, robbing her of coherent thought for a bit too long. At the last minute, she remembered to turn the wheel so Duke would angle into the drive.

Stumbling from the cab, she hoped Zach hadn't noticed how much he'd unsettled her usual calm, take-the-road-of-least-resistance approach to life. Lucy grabbed her hand, and despite her protests, Alice found herself across the roomy kitchen table from the impetuous girl, while Zach grilled ham and cheese sandwiches at the stove.

It was John's, "You have to eat. You may as well eat with us," that tempted her.

"My dad's a great cook," Lucy had weighed in.

Against her better judgment, Alice lost the argument to keep her distance. It was Zach's pinched expression at the invitation that finally convinced her to take his grandfather up on the offer.

Deep down, where she let no one see, she wondered what it was about this man, of the few she'd met in her travels, that made her aware of things she didn't want to feel again.

For her peace of mind, she needed to stay far away from Sexy Guy and his charming family. Nothing good would come of getting chummy with this hot stranger.

"Do you sleep in the caravan?" The girl's curiosity was endless.

"Sometimes."

"Sweet!"

Zach put plates of golden sandwiches and sliced apples in the middle of the table. "Go wash your hands, Luce. And while you're back there, tell Granddad dinner's on the table."

Sexy Guy stayed where he was for a long minute after his daughter left, making Alice's nerves tingle – in a good way, dang it. "Can I...um...set the table or something?"

"I'm sorry I was rude earlier." The apology came out slowly in an attention-grabbing baritone, layered with just the right amount of regret. "I have a hard time keeping staff."

Alice's stomach did a funny little somersault.

Unable to sit still under his sheepish gaze, she headed for the cupboards looking for plates and napkins. The kitchen sparkled. Through the archway, the living area was neat as a pin. Men didn't usually live that way, and neither did pre-teen girls. "You have staff?"

"We have four residents, including my granddad, living here at Martha's Elder House. Penelope managed the house. Blake was our driver and handyman."

"And John and Lucy didn't like them." An easy assumption.

"Where are you planning to stay tonight?" he asked at the same time, putting the table between them.

Alice was glad for the subconscious message. She didn't want to be tempted. Married once, with what she thought was a bright future ahead of them, she'd learned her lesson the hard way. As appealing as it might be to hang around long enough to get to know the handsome single dad, she didn't need any reason to stay in Sellwood once she'd replaced Duke's fuel pump.

She sighed regretfully. They were two ships passing in the night. Too bad. Still, her traitorous pulse pounded out a beat like a high school cheerleader. *Zach, Zach, he's our man...*

"Caravan." The word came out sharper than she intended. Sexy Guy watched her, curiosity changing his expression into something much more diverting. She softened her tone. "I'll stay in the caravan."

His granddad, John, he'd introduced himself as, came into the kitchen with Lucy right behind him. "No, you won't. With Penelope and Blake gone, we have two empty rooms in the basement. You can stay in one of them until your truck is fixed."

She shook her head. "I don't want to put you out—" Or stay too long under the same roof with the family that belonged to Sexy Guy.

John shot a pointed look at Zach. That couldn't be good. "You're not putting us out, is she, Zach?"

Looking uncomfortable, Zach shrugged. "No. Of course, you're not."

Lucy grabbed her hand. "Stay with us. Dad, tell her she has to stay."

"You're welcome to stay," he obliged his daughter, eyes twinkling briefly as though enjoying a private joke at Alice's expense.

Dang it. Grace under fire. Another point in his good guy tally.

Lucy let go of Alice and shoved her hands in her pants pockets. "We would like it if you'd stay."

We? She highly doubted that. And where had the girl learned to negotiate like a sixteen-year-old in a twelve-year-old's body?

"Lucy, sit down and eat your dinner, and leave Ms. York alone. She'll stay if she wants." The unapologetic mischief was gone. Zach scrubbed the counter by the stove as though he'd made a huge mess while making dinner.

Alice *wished* things could be different. "I can't. Really."

Zach stopped scrubbing, his intense gaze landing on her

face. He still looked rattled, but he said gruffly, "You can."

Oh, good grief. At least now she knew where his daughter got her powers of persuasion.

Alice gave in. Reluctantly. She couldn't fight all three of them.

"Thanks for the offer." *Push and shove was more like it.* "I'll stay. But only until Tuesday or Wednesday when I get Duke going again."

A Fool for Love
Amazon | BN | Apple Books | Kobo

About The Author

Susan Lute is an award-winning author and hopeful day-dreamer who writes bold, brave, and heart-stirring stories that blur the lines between romance, women's fiction, and a dash of the fantastical. Whether it's a small-town love story or a sweeping romantasy with dragon-marked heroes and fire-kissed destinies, her tales are always rooted in courage, connection, and a spark of magic.

When she's not conjuring worlds with her pen, you'll find her sipping that sacred first cup of coffee, wandering through her garden, chasing light with her camera, or adding one more finishing touch to the house she's turned into a haven over the past thirty years. She believes in second chances, found families, and that love—of all kinds—is the most powerful magic of all.

Other books by Susan Lute

Strawberry Ridge Ranch Romance
The Prodigal Cowboy Returns
The Cowboy Fix
The Rancher's Heart

Angel Point Romance
The Sheriff's Baby Bargain
Wanted by the Marshal
The Christmas Makeover
The Valentine Project
The Fake Marriage Proposal

A Wally Creek Novel
The Little Tea Room on River Road

A Sellwood Novella
A Fool For Love
A Merry Little Sellwood Christmas, A Sellwood Short

Sealed With A Kiss
Love Lessons

Falling For a Hero
A Girl Named Jane
Jane's Long March Home
A Marine's Christmas Proposal, A Short Story

Rosewood Romance
The Return of Benjamin Quincy
Be My Valentine? A Rosewood Short

The London Affair
The Broken Road

Oops…We're Married? A Silhouette Romance Classic

Where to Buy

Amazon | B&N | Apple Books | Rakuten Kobo | Google Play

Also available in the UK

What Others Have to Say

"**A** heartwarming [and] truly riveting story with beautiful characters and a plot you won't soon forget." ~ RT Book Reviews

"*A timely story that will appeal to those seeking a sweet story of finding yourself again.*" ~ Night Owl Reviews

"*An engaging romance about how love can change dreams.*" ~ RT Book Reviews

"*Susan Lute has created a charming novel filled with meddling relatives and friends, bad decisions, good decisions, flawed people, and passionate love. These are real people. No silly flippant girls or muscle bound men. These people have problems brought on because they thought they were doing what was best for the person they loved. Add an emotionally fragile 10 year old girl who needs them and you have this wonderful story.*" ~ Amazon Review

"*Susan Lute created a wonderful cast of characters and a charming town to help tell the story of finding your true happiness. I think each of us can find a little piece of Sydney in ourselves.*" ~ Cocktails and Books

"*This was a highly enjoyable read. The story fit right into what I like to read in my contemporary romances.*" ~ Amazon Review

"*Beautifully written, The London Affair by Susan Lute is the story of the inner workings of a complicated family and the hope of new beginnings. Read this book with a box of tissues.*" ~ Night Owl Reviews

"*Susan Lute is a beautiful keeper of the human heart. She explores the soul and leaves the reader certain life is worth the journey.*" ~ Amazon Review